Five Have A Mystery To Solve

Enid Blyton

THE FAMOUS FIVE

Five Have A Mystery To Solve

Hodder
Children's
Books

A division of Hachette Children's Books

Enid Blyton ® Famous Five ® Copyright © 2011 Chorion Rights Ltd
All rights reserved
'Foreword' copyright Sophie Smallwood 2010

First published in Great Britain in 1963 by Hodder and Stoughton

This revised edition first published in 2011 by Hodder Children's Books

With thanks to Rachel Elliot

The right of Enid Blyton to be identified as the Author of
the Work has been asserted by her in accordance with the
Copyright, Designs and Patents Act 1988.

2

A Catalogue record for this book is available from the British Library

ISBN 978 0 340 93178 3

Typeset in Sabon by Avon DataSet Ltd, Bidford-on-Avon, Warwickshire

Printed and bound in Great Britain by Clays Ltd, St Ives plc

The paper and board used in this paperback by Hodder Children's Books
are natural recyclable products made from wood grown in sustainable
forests. The manufacturing processes conform to the environmental
regulations of the country of origin.

Hodder Children's Books
a division of Hachette Children's Books
338 Euston Road, London NW1 3BH
An Hachette UK company
www.hachette.co.uk

Contents

1 Easter holidays

'The nicest word in the English language is holidays!' said Dick, helping himself to a large spoonful of marmalade. 'Pass the toast, Anne. Mum, do you feel downhearted to have us all tearing about the place again?'

'Of course not,' said his mother. 'The only thing that *really* worries me when holidays come, is Food – Food with a capital F. We never seem to have enough in the house when all three of you are back. And by the way – does anyone know what's happened to the sausages that were in the larder?'

'Sausages – sausages – let me think!' said Julian, frowning. Anne gave a sudden giggle. She knew quite well what had happened.

'Well, Mum – you said we could get our own meal last night, as you were out,' said Julian. 'So we poked about and decided on sausages.'

'Yes, but Julian – two *whole* packets of

sausages!' said his mother. 'I know Georgina came over to spend the evening – but even so . . . !'

'She brought *Timmy*,' said Anne. '*He* likes sausages too, Mum.'

'Well, that's the last time I leave the larder door unlocked, when I go out!' said her mother. 'Imagine cooking those lovely pork sausages for a *dog* – especially Timmy, with his enormous appetite! Really, Anne! I meant to have them for our lunch today.'

'Well – we thought we'd go and spend the day at Kirrin, with George and Timmy,' said Dick. 'That's if you don't want us for anything, Mum.'

'I *do* want you,' said his mother. 'Mrs Layman is coming to tea, and she said she wants to see you about something.'

The three groaned, and Dick protested at once. 'Oh *Mum* – the first day of the holidays – and we have to be in for tea! It's not fair – a glorious spring day like this, too!'

'Oh – we'll be in for tea all right,' said Julian, giving Dick a sharp little kick under the table, as he saw his mother's disappointed face. 'Mrs Layman's nice – she's been really kind since we moved near to Kirrin.'

'And she gave me a present last birthday,' said Anne. 'Do you think we could ask George over too – with Timmy? George'll be really disappointed if we aren't with her the first day of the holidays.'

'Yes, of course you can,' said her mother. 'Go and ring her up now, and arrange it. And don't forget to put our old Tibby-cat in the shed, with a saucer of milk. She's scared stiff of Timmy – he's so enormous. And please, all of you, TRY to look clean at tea-time.'

'*I'll* see to Dick and Anne,' said Julian, with a grin. 'I must remember to find their overalls!'

'I'm going to phone George now, this minute,' said Anne, getting up from the table. 'Do you mind, Mum? I've finished – and I'd like to catch George before she takes Tim for a walk, or does some shopping for Aunt Fanny.'

'Uncle Quentin will be glad to be rid of George, even for a meal,' said Dick. 'He fell over her lacrosse stick yesterday, and wanted to know why she left her *fishing* net about! George didn't know what he was talking about!'

'Poor Georgina,' said his mother. 'It's a pity that both she and her dad have exactly the same hot tempers. Her mum must find it difficult to keep the peace! Ah – here's Anne back again. Did you get George on the phone?'

'Yes. She's thrilled,' said Anne. 'She says it's just as well we're not going to spend the day with her, because Uncle Quentin has lost some papers he was working on, and he's turning the house upside down. George said she'll probably be mad as a hatter by the time she arrives this afternoon! Uncle Quentin even made Aunt Fanny turn out her knitting bag to see if the papers were there!'

'Dear Quentin,' said her mother. 'Such a truly brilliant scientist – remembers every book he's ever read – every paper he's ever written – and has the finest brain I know – and yet loses some valuable paper or other almost every week!'

'He loses something else every day of the week too,' said Dick, with a grin. 'His temper! Poor George – she's always in some sort of trouble!'

'Well, anyway, she's really glad to be coming over here!' said Anne. 'She's biking over, with Timmy. She'll be here for lunch. Is that all right, Mum?'

'Of course!' said her mother. 'Now – seeing that you had today's dinner for last night's supper, you'd better do a little shopping for me. What shall we have?'

'SAUSAGES!' said everyone, at once.

'I'd have thought you were quite literally *fed up* with sausages, after last night's feast,' said their mother, laughing. 'All right – sausages. But Timmy can have a bone – a nice meaty bone. I am NOT going to buy any more sausages for him, that's quite certain.'

'And shall we get some nice cakes for tea as Mrs Layman is coming?' said Anne. 'Or are you going to make some, Mum?'

'I'll make a few buns,' said her mother. 'And you can choose whatever else you like – as long as you don't buy up the shop!'

The three went off shopping, cycling along the lane to the village. It was truly a lovely spring day. The celandines were golden in the ditches, and daisies were scattered everywhere. Dick burst into song as they went, and the cows in the nearby fields lifted their heads in surprise as Dick's loud voice swept round them.

Anne laughed. It was good to be with her brothers again. She missed them very much when she was away at school. And now they would have almost a whole month together with their cousin George too. She was suddenly overwhelmed with joy, and lifted up her voice and joined Dick in his singing. Her brothers looked at her with affection and amusement.

'Good old Anne,' said Dick. 'You're such a quiet little mouse, it's nice to hear you singing so loudly.'

'I am NOT a quiet little mouse!' said Anne, surprised and rather hurt. 'What makes you say that? You just wait – you may get a surprise one day!'

'Yes – we may!' said Julian. 'But I doubt it. A mouse can't suddenly turn into a tiger! Anyway, one tiger's enough. *George* is the tiger of our family – she can put out her claws all right – and roar – and rant and rave!'

Everyone laughed at the picture of George as a tiger. Dick wobbled as he laughed and his front wheel touched Anne's back wheel. She turned round fiercely.

'LOOK OUT, IDIOT! You nearly had me over! Can't you see where you're going? Be sensible, can't you?'

'Hey, Anne – whatever's the matter?' said

Julian, amazed to hear his gentle little sister lashing out so suddenly.

Anne laughed. 'It's all right. I was just being a tiger for a moment – putting out my claws! I thought Dick and you might like to see them!'

'Well, well!' said Dick, riding beside her, 'I've never heard you yell like that before. Surprising – but quite pleasing! What about you showing George your claws sometime when she gets out of hand?'

'Stop teasing,' said Anne. 'Here's the butcher's. For goodness' sake go and get the sausages, and be sensible. I'll go and buy the cakes.'

The baker's shop was full of new-made buns and cakes, and smelt deliciously of home-made bread. Anne enjoyed herself choosing a vast selection.

'After all,' she thought, 'there'll be eight of us – counting Timmy – and if we're all hungry, cakes soon disappear.'

The boys were very pleased to see all the paper bags.

'Looks like a good tea today,' said Dick. 'I hope the old lady – what's her name? – Layman – who's coming to tea today, has a good appetite. I wonder what she's going to tell us about.'

'Did you buy a nice meaty bone for Timmy?' asked Anne. 'He'll like that for his tea.'

'We bought such a beauty that I'm pretty sure Mum'll say it's good enough to make soup from,' said Dick, with a grin. 'So I'll keep it in my saddlebag till he comes. Dear Tim. He deserves a really good bone. Best dog I ever knew!'

'He's been on a lot of adventures with us,' said Anne, cycling beside the boys, as the road was empty. 'And he seemed to enjoy them all.'

'Yes. So did we!' said Dick. 'Well – who knows? An adventure may be lying in wait for us these holidays too! I seem to smell one in the air!'

'You don't!' said Anne. 'You're just making that up. *I'd* like a bit of peace after a hectic term at school. I worked really hard this last term.'

'Well – you were top of your form, and captain of games – so you deserve to have the kind of holiday you like,' said Julian, proud of his young sister. 'And so you shall! Adventures are OUT! Do you hear that, Dick? We keep absolutely clear of them. So that's that!'

'Is it, Ju?' said Anne, laughing. 'Well – we'll see!'

2 *A visitor to tea*

George and Timmy were waiting for Julian, Dick and Anne when they arrived home. Timmy was standing in the road, ears pricked, long tail waving. He went quite mad when he saw their bikes rounding the corner, and galloped towards them at top speed, barking madly, much to the horror of a boy carrying a large basket.

The boy disappeared into the nearest garden at top speed, yelling 'Mad dog, mad dog!' Timmy tore past, and forced the three to dismount, for they were afraid of knocking him over.

'*Dear* Timmy!' said Anne, patting the excited dog. 'Please put your tongue in – I'm sure it'll fall out some day!'

Timmy ran to each of them in turn, woofing in delight, licking everyone, and altogether behaving as if he hadn't seen them for a year!

'Now that's enough, boy,' said Dick, pushing him away, and trying to mount his bike once more. 'After all, we did see you yesterday. Where's George?'

George had heard Timmy barking, and had now run out too. The three cycled up to her, and she grinned happily at them.

'Hello! You've been shopping, I see. Shut up barking, Timmy, you talk too much. Sorry you couldn't come over to Kirrin Cottage – but I'm really glad you asked me to come to *you* – my dad still hasn't found the papers he's lost, and honestly, our place is like a madhouse – cupboards being turned out, even the kitchen store cupboard – and I left poor Mum up in the loft, looking there – although *why* Dad should think they might be there, I don't know!'

'Poor George – I can see your dad tearing his hair, and shouting, and all the time he's probably put the papers into the bin by mistake!' said Dick, with a chuckle.

'Oh – we never *thought* of that!' said George. 'I'd better phone Mum at once, and tell her to look. Bright idea of yours, Dick.'

'Well, you go and phone, and we'll put our bikes away,' said Julian. 'Take your nose away from that bag of sausages, Timmy. You're in disgrace over sausages, let me tell you. You're suspected of eating too many last night!'

'He did eat rather a lot,' said George. 'I took my eye off him, and he wolfed quite a few. Hey, who's this Mrs Layman who's coming to tea? Have we *got* to stay in and have tea with her? I hoped we might be going off for a picnic this afternoon.'

''Fraid not,' said Dick, 'Mrs Layman is apparently coming to talk to us about something. So we have to be in – with clean hands, nice manners, and everything. So behave yourself, George!'

George gave him a friendly punch. 'That's unfair,' said Dick. 'You should have seen Anne this morning, George – yelled at me like a tiger howling, and showed her teeth, and—'

'Don't be an idiot, Dick,' said Anne. 'He called me a mouse, George – he said we had *one* tiger – you – and that was enough in the family. So I went for him – put out my claws for a moment, and gave him such a surprise. I quite liked it!'

'Good old Anne!' said George, amused. 'But you're not really cut out to be a tiger, and rage and roar, you know.'

'I could be, if I had to,' said Anne, obstinately. 'One of these days I'll surprise you all. You just wait!'

'All right. We will,' said Julian, putting his arm round his sister. 'Come on, now – we'd better get indoors before Timmy gets some of the cakes out of the bags. Stop licking that bag, Tim – you'll make a hole in it.'

'He can smell the cherry buns inside,' said Anne. 'Shall I give him one?'

'NO!' said Julian. 'Cherry buns are wasted on him, you know that. Don't you remember how he chews the bun apart and spits out the cherries?'

'Woof,' said Timmy, exactly as if he agreed. He went to sniff at the bag with his bone inside.

'That's your dinner, Tim,' said Anne. 'Plenty of meat on it, too. Look, there's Mum at the window, beckoning. I expect she wants the sausages. NO, Timmy – the sausages are not for you. Get down! I never in my life knew such a hungry dog. Anybody would think you starved him, George.'

'Well, they'd think wrong, then,' said George. 'Timmy, come to heel.'

Timmy came, still looking round longingly

at the various bags that the others were now taking from their saddlebags.

They all went indoors, and deposited the goods on the kitchen table. Doris, the lady who helped their mother in the holidays, opened the bags and looked inside, keeping a sharp eye on Timmy.

'Better take that dog of yours out of my kitchen,' she said. 'Funny how sausages always disappear when he's around. Get down, now – take your paws off my clean table!'

Timmy trotted out of the kitchen. He thought it was a pity that cooks didn't like him. He liked *them* very much indeed – they always smelt so deliciously of cooking, and there were always so many titbits around which he longed for, but was seldom offered. Ah well – he'd trot into the kitchen again when Doris had gone upstairs for something! He might perhaps find a few bits and pieces on the floor then!

'Hello, Georgina!' said her aunt, coming into the kitchen, Timmy following her in delight. 'Timmy, go out of the kitchen. I don't trust you within a mile of sausages. Go on – shoo!'

Timmy 'shooed'. He liked Anne's mother, but knew that when she said 'Shoo!' she meant it. He lay down on a rug in the living room, with a heavy sigh, wondering how long it would be before he had that lovely meaty bone. He put his head on his paws, and kept his ears pricked for George. He thought it very unfair that George shouldn't be shooed out of the kitchen too.

'Now, for goodness' sake keep out of my way while I cook the lunch,' said Doris to the children milling round her kitchen. 'And shut the door, please. I don't want that great hungry dog sniffing round me all the time, making out he's starving, when he's as fat as butter!'

'He's NOT!' said George, indignantly. 'Timmy has never been fat in his life. He's not that kind of dog. He's *never* greedy!'

'Well, he must be the first dog ever born that wasn't greedy,' said Doris. 'Can't trust any of them! There was that pug dog of Mrs Lane's – crunched up lumps of sugar whenever it could reach a sugar bowl – and that fat poodle next door – came and knocked over the cream that the milkman left outside the back door – *deliberately* knocked it over, mark you – and then licked up every drop. Ha – his mistress tried to make out he didn't like cream – but you should have seen his nose – covered in cream up to his eyes!'

Timmy looked in at the kitchen door, his nose in the air, for all the world as if he were deeply offended at Doris's remarks. Julian laughed.

'You've wounded his pride, Doris!' he said.

'I'll wound him somewhere else, too, if he comes sniffing round me when I'm cooking,' said Doris. That made George give one of her scowls, but the others couldn't help laughing!

The morning went very pleasantly. The Five went down to the beach and walked round the high cliffs, enjoying the stiff breeze that blew in their faces. Timmy raced after every seagull that dared to sit on the smooth sand, annoyed that each one rose up lazily on great wings as soon as he almost reached it.

They were all hungry for their dinner, and not one single morsel was left when they had finished! Doris had made a tremendous steamed pudding, with lashings of treacle, which was, as usual, a huge success.

'Wish I had a tongue like Timmy's and could lick up the lovely treacle left on the bottom of the dish,' said George. 'Such a waste!'

'You certainly won't be able to eat any tea, I'm

sure of that!' said her aunt.

But, of course, she was wrong. When tea-time came they all felt quite ready for it, and were very impatient when Mrs Layman was late!

The tea looked lovely, laid on a big table covered with a white lace cloth. The children sat and looked at it longingly. When would Mrs Layman arrive?

'I begin to feel I'm not going to like Mrs Layman,' said George, at last. 'I can't *bear* looking at those cream cakes when I'm hungry.'

The front door bell rang. Hurray! Then in came a cheerful, smiling old lady nodding to everyone, very pleased to see such a nice little party waiting for her.

'Here's Mrs Layman, children,' said Julian's mother. 'Sit down, Mrs Layman. We're delighted to have you.'

'Well, I've come to ask the children something,' said Mrs Layman. 'But we'll have tea first, and then I'll say what I've come to say. My, my – what a wonderful tea! I'm glad I feel hungry!'

Everyone else was hungry too, and soon the bread and butter, the sandwiches, the buns, the cakes and everything else disappeared. Timmy sat quietly by George, who slipped him a titbit now and again when no one was looking. Mrs Layman chatted away. She was a very interesting person, and the children liked her very much.

'Well now,' she said, when tea was finished, 'I'm sure you must be wanting to know why I asked to come to tea today. I wanted to ask your mum, Julian, if there was any chance of you three . . . and this other boy here, what's his name – George! . . . would you like to help me out of a difficulty?'

Nobody pointed out that George was a girl, not a boy, and that George was short for Georgina. George, as usual, was pleased to be taken for a boy. They all looked at Mrs Layman, listening to her with interest.

'It's like this,' she said. 'I've a dear little house up on the hills, overlooking the harbour – and I've a grandson staying with me there – Wilfrid. Well, I have to go to look after a cousin of mine, who's ill – and Wilfrid can't bear to be left alone. I just wondered if your mum would allow you children to share the little house with Wilfrid, and, well keep him company. He feels a bit scared being on his own. There's a nice woman there, who comes in to cook and clean – but poor Wilfrid's really scared of being in such a lonely place, high up on the hill.'

'You mean that lovely little house with the wonderful view?' said Julian's mother.

'Yes. It's rather *primitive* in some ways – no water laid on, only just a well to use – and no electricity or gas – just candles, or an oil-lamp. Maybe it sounds too old-fashioned for words – but honestly the view makes up for it! Perhaps the children would like to come over and see it, before they decide?'

Mrs Layman looked earnestly round at everyone, and nobody knew quite what to say.

'Well – we'll *certainly* come and see it,' said Julian's mother. 'And if the children feel like it, well, they can stay there. They do like being on their own, of course.'

'Yes,' said Julian. 'We'll come and see it, Mrs Layman. Mum's going to be busy with a bazaar soon – she'll be glad to get us out of the way – and, of course, we *do* like being on our own!'

Mrs Layman looked extremely pleased.

'Tomorrow, then?' she said. 'About ten o'clock. You'll love the view. Wonderful, wonderful!

You can see right over the great harbour, and for miles around. Well – I must be going now. I'll tell Wilfrid you children may be keeping him company. He's *such* a nice lad – so helpful. You'll love him.'

Julian had his doubts about the nice, helpful Wilfrid. He even wondered if Mrs Layman wanted to get away from Wilfrid, and leave him to himself! No – that was too silly. Anyway, they'd soon see what the place was like, tomorrow.

'It *would* be fun to be on our own again,' said George, when Mrs Layman had gone. 'I don't expect this Wilfrid would be any bother. He's probably just a silly kid, scared of being left alone – although apparently there *is* a woman there! Well – we'll go tomorrow! Maybe the view will make up for dear Wilfrid!'

3 The cottage on the hill
– and Wilfrid

Next day the children prepared to go and see the cottage belonging to Mrs Layman.

'You coming too, Mum?' asked Julian. 'We'd like your advice!'

'Well no, dear,' said his mother. 'I've rather a lot to do – there's a meeting on at the village hall, and I promised to go to it.'

'You're full of good works, Mum,' said Julian, giving her a hug. 'All right, we'll go by ourselves. I expect we'll know at once whether we'd like to stay in the cottage – or not. Also, we MUST know what this Wilfrid is like! It's quarter to ten, and George is already here, with Timmy. I'll call the others and we'll get our bikes.'

Soon the four were on their bikes, with Timmy, as usual, running alongside, his long tongue out, his eyes bright and happy. This was Timmy's idea of perfect happiness – to be with the four children all day long!

They went along a road that ran on the top of a hill. They swung round a corner – and there, spread far below them, was a great sea vista that included a wonderful harbour, filled with big and little ships. The sea was as blue as the Mediterranean, quite breathtaking. Anne jumped off her bike at once.

'I must just feast my eyes on all this before I go any further!' she said. 'What a panorama! What miles of sea and sky!'

She put her bike against a gate and then climbed over and stood by herself, gazing down at the view. Dick joined her.

Then suddenly a voice shouted loudly, 'FORE! FORE!'

A small white thing came whizzing through the air and landed just by Anne's foot. She jumped in surprise.

'It's a golf ball,' said Dick. 'No, don't pick it up. Whoever's playing with it has to come and hit it from exactly where it fell. Good thing you weren't hit, Anne. I didn't realise that this gate led on to a golf course!'

'We ought to have a walk over it,' said Anne.

'Just look at those gorse bushes over there, absolutely flaming with yellow blossom – and all the tiny flowers springing up everywhere – speedwell and coltsfoot and daisies and celandines – beautiful. And what a view!'

'Yes – and if Mrs Layman's cottage has a view anything like this, I'd definitely like to stay there!' said Dick. 'Think of getting out of bed in the morning and seeing this enormous view out of the window – the harbour – the sea beyond – the hills all around – the great spread of sky . . .'

'You ought to be a poet, Dick!' said Anne, in surprise.

The golfers came up at that moment, and the children stood aside and watched one of them take aim at the ball, and then strike it easily and strongly. The ball soared through the air, and landed far away on a smooth green fairway.

'Good shot!' said the man's partner, and the two sauntered off together.

'Funny game, really,' said Anne. 'Just hitting a ball all round the course.'

'Wish I had some clubs!' said Dick. 'I'm sure I could hit some fantastic shots!'

'Well, if that cottage is anywhere near the

golf course perhaps you could pay to have a lesson,' said Anne. 'I bet you could hit a ball as far as that man!'

The others were now yelling for them to come back, so they went to fetch their bikes. Soon they were all riding along the road again.

'We have to look for a small white gate, with "Hill Cottage" painted on it,' said George. 'On the hillside facing the sea.'

'There it is!' cried Anne. 'We'll pile our bikes together against the hedge, and go in at the gate.'

They left their bikes in a heap and went through the gate. Not far to their left stood a funny old cottage, its back to them, its front looking down the steep hill that ran towards the great harbour and the sea beyond.

'It's like a cottage out of an old fairy tale,' said Anne. 'Funny little chimneys, crooked walls, a thatched roof, all uneven – and what tiny windows!'

They walked down a little winding path that led to the cottage. They soon came to a well, and leant over it to see the water deep down.

'So that's the water we'd have to drink!' said

Anne, wrinkling up her nose. 'And we'd have to let down the bucket by winding this handle – and down it would go on the rope! Do you think the water's pure?'

'Well, seeing that people must have drunk it for years on end – the ones living in that cottage, anyway – I should think it's all right!' said Julian. 'Come on – let's find the front door of the cottage – if it has one!'

It had a wooden door, hung rather crooked, with an old brass knocker. It faced down the hill, and was flanked on each side by small windows. Two other small windows were above. Julian looked at them. The bedrooms would be very small, he thought – would there *really* be room for them all?

He knocked at the door. Nobody came to open it. He knocked again, and then looked for a bell, but there wasn't one.

'See if the door's unlocked,' said Anne.

So Julian turned the handle – and at once the door gave under his hand! It opened straight into a room that looked like a kitchen-living room.

Julian gave a shout. 'Anyone at home?'

There was no answer.

'Well – as this is obviously the cottage we were meant to see, we'd better go in,' said Julian and in they all went.

It was old, very old. The carved wooden furniture was old too. Ancient oil-lamps stood on two tables in the room, and in a recess there was an oil-stove with a saucepan on top. A narrow, crooked stairway made of wood curved up to the floor above. Julian went up, and found himself in a long, darkish room, its roof thatched with reed and held up by black beams.

'This place must be hundreds of years old!' he called down to the others. 'I don't think it's big enough for us four and the others too – Wilfrid and the helper.'

Just as he finished calling down the stairs, the front door was flung open and someone came in.

'What are you doing here?' he shouted. 'This is *my* cottage!'

Julian went quickly down the stairs, and there, facing them all, stood a boy of about ten, a scowl on his brown face.

'Er – are you Wilfrid, by any chance?' asked Dick, politely.

'Yes, I am. And who are you? And where's my

grandmother? She'll soon chuck you out!' said the boy.

'Is your grandmother Mrs Layman?' asked Julian. 'If so, she asked us to come and see her cottage, and decide if we'd like to keep you company. She said she had to go away and look after a sick relative.'

'Well, I don't want you!' said the boy. 'So go away. I'm all right here alone. My grandmother's a nuisance, always fussing around.'

'I thought there was a lady who looks after you too,' said Julian. 'Where is she?'

'She only comes in the morning, and I sent her off,' said Wilfrid. 'She left me some food. I want to be alone. I don't want *you*. So go away.'

'Don't be an idiot, Wilfrid,' said Julian. 'You can't live all alone here. You're just a kid.'

'I won't be living all alone. I've plenty of friends,' said Wilfrid, defiantly.

'You CAN'T have plenty of friends here in this lonely place, with only the hills and sky around you,' said Dick.

'Well, I *have*!' said Wilfrid. 'And here's one – so look out!' And, to their horror, he put his hand into his pocket, and brought out a snake!

Anne screamed, and tried to hide behind Julian. Wilfrid saw her fright and came towards her, holding the snake by its middle, so that it swayed to and fro, its bright little eyes gleaming.

'Don't be scared, Anne,' said Julian. 'It's only a harmless grass snake. Put the creature back into your pocket, Wilfrid, and don't play the fool. If that snake's the only friend you have, you'll be pretty lonely here by yourself!'

'I've *plenty* of friends, I tell you!' shouted Wilfrid, stuffing the snake back into his pocket. 'I'll hit you if you don't believe me.'

'Oh no, you won't,' said Dick. 'Just show us your other friends. If they're kids like you, it's just too bad!'

'Kids? I don't make friends with *kids*!' said Wilfrid, scornfully. '*I'll* show you I'm telling the truth. Come out here on the hillside, and see some of my other friends.'

They all trooped out of the little cottage, on to the hillside, amazed at this fierce, strange boy. When they were in the open, they saw that he had eyes as bright blue as the speedwell in the grass, and hair almost as yellow as the celandines.

'Sit down and keep quiet,' he ordered. 'Over

there, by that bush. And don't move a finger. I'll
soon make you believe in my friends! How dare
you come here, doubting my word!'

They all sat down obediently beside the gorse
bush, puzzled and rather amused. The boy sat
down too, and drew something out of his pocket.
What was it? George tried to see, but it was half
hidden in his right hand.

He put it to his mouth, and began to whistle. It
was a soft, weird whistle that grew loud and
then died away again. There was no tune, no
melody, just a kind of beautiful dirge that pulled
at the heart.

'Sad,' thought Anne, 'such a sad little tune – if
you could *call* it a tune!'

Something stirred a little way down the hill –
and then to everyone's astonishment, an animal
appeared – a hare! Its great ears stood upright, its
big eyes stared straight at the boy with the strange
little pipe. Then the hare lolloped right up to
Wilfrid – and began to dance! Soon another came,
but this one only watched. The first one then
seemed to go mad, and leapt about wildly, utterly
unafraid.

The tune changed a little – and a rabbit

appeared. Then another and another. One came to Wilfrid's feet and sniffed at them, its whiskers quivering. Then it lay down against the boy's foot.

A bird flew down – a beautiful magpie! It stood nearby, watching the hare, fascinated. It took no notice of the children at all. They all held their breath, amazed and delighted.

And then Timmy gave a little growl, deep down in his throat. He didn't really mean to, but he just couldn't help it! At once the hares, the rabbits and the magpie fled, the magpie squawking in fright.

Wilfrid faced round at once, his eyes blazing. He lifted his hand to strike Timmy – but George caught his fist at once.

'Let go!' yelled Wilfrid. 'That dog scared my friends! I'll get a stick and whip him. He's the worst dog in the world, he's—'

And then something strange happened. Timmy came gently over to Wilfrid, lay down, and put his head on the angry boy's knee, looking up at him lovingly. The boy, his hand still raised to strike, lowered it, and stroked Timmy's head, making a strange crooning noise.

'Timmy! Come here!' ordered George, amazed and angry.

To think that *her* dog, her very *own* dog, should go to a boy who had been about to strike him! Timmy stood up, gave Wilfrid a lick, and went to George.

The boy watched him, and then spoke to them all.

'You *can* come and stay in my cottage,' he said, 'if you'll bring that dog too. There aren't many dogs like him – he's a *wonderful* dog. I'd like him for one of my friends.'

Then, without another word, Wilfrid sprang up and ran away down the hill, leaving four very astonished people – and a dog who whined dismally because the boy had gone. Well, well, Timmy – there must indeed be something about that boy, if you stand looking after him as if you had lost one of your very best friends!

4 Settling in

The Five stared after Wilfrid in silence. Timmy wagged his tail and whined. He wanted the boy to come back.

'Well, thank you, Timmy,' said Anne, patting the big dog on the head. 'We certainly wouldn't have had this lovely little cottage, with its incredible view, if you hadn't made friends with Wilfrid. What a funny boy he is!'

'A bit strange, *I* think!' said George, still amazed at the way that Timmy had gone to Wilfrid, when the boy had been about to strike him. 'I'm not sure that I like him!'

'Don't be silly, George,' said Dick, who had been very much impressed by the boy's handling of the hares, the rabbits and the magpie. 'That boy must have a wonderful love for animals. They would never come to him like that, if they didn't trust him absolutely. Anyone who loves animals like he does must be all right.'

'I bet I could make them come to *me* if I had that pipe,' said George, making up her mind to borrow it if she could.

Anne went back into the cottage. She was delighted with it.

'It must be very, very old,' she thought. 'It stands dreaming here all day long, full of memories of the people who have lived here and loved it. And how they must all have loved this view – miles and miles of heather, great stretches of sea – and the biggest, highest widest sky I've ever seen. It's a happy place. Even the clouds seem happy – they're scurrying along, so white against the blue!'

She explored the cottage thoroughly. She decided that the room above, under the thatch, should be for the three boys. There were two mattresses – one small, one larger. 'The little one for Wilfrid – the big one for Dick and Julian,' she thought. 'And George and I can sleep down in the living room, with Tim on guard. I wonder if there are any rugs we could sleep on. Ah – wait a bit – this couch is a pull-out bed – just right for us two girls! Good!'

Anne enjoyed herself thoroughly. This was the

kind of problem she liked – fixing up this and that for the others! She found a little larder, facing north. It had a few tins in it, and a jug of milk, slightly sour. It also had two loaves of extremely stale bread, and a tin of rather hard cakes.

'Mrs Layman doesn't seem to be a very good housekeeper for herself and Wilfrid,' thought Anne, seriously. 'We'll have to go down to the village and get a stock of decent food. I might get a small ham – the boys would like that. Oh – this *is* going to be fun!'

Julian came to the door to see what she was doing. When he saw her happy, serious face, he chuckled.

'Acting "mum" to us, as usual?' he said. 'Deciding who's going to sleep where, and which of us is to do the shopping, and which the washing up? Dear Anne – what would we do without you when we go off on our own?'

'I love it,' said Anne, happily. 'Julian, we need another rug or two, and a pillow, and some food. And . . .'

'Well, we'll have to go back home and collect a few clothes and other things,' said Julian. 'We can shop on the way back, and get whatever we want.

I wonder if that woman that Mrs Layman spoke about will be coming in to help?'

'Well – Wilfrid said he sent her off,' said Anne. 'And I think perhaps as the cottage is so small, it might be better if we managed it ourselves. I think I could do a bit of cooking on that oil-stove in the corner – and anyway we can pretty well live on cold stuff, you know – ham and salad and cheese and fruit. It'd be easy enough for any of us to pop down to the village on our bikes, to fetch anything we needed.'

'Listen!' said Julian, cocking his head to one side. 'Is that somebody calling us?'

Yes – it was. When Julian went outside, he saw Mrs Layman at the gate that led on to the hillside where the cottage stood. He went over to her.

'We LOVE the cottage!' he said. 'And if it's all right, we'd like to move in today. We can easily pop home and bring back anything we want. It's a glorious old place, isn't it – and the view must be the best anywhere!'

'Well, that harbour is the second biggest stretch of water in the whole world,' said Mrs Layman. 'The only stretch that's any bigger is Sydney harbour – so you have something to feast your eyes on, Julian!'

'Definitely!' said Julian. 'It's amazing – and so *very* blue! I only wish I could paint – but I can't. At least, not very well!'

'What about Wilfrid?' said Mrs Layman, anxiously. 'Is he behaving himself? He's – well – he's rather a *difficult* boy at times. And he can be very rude. He hasn't any brothers to rub off his awkward corners, you see.'

'Oh, don't you worry about Wilfrid!' said Julian, cheerfully. 'He'll have to toe the line, and do as he's told. We all do our bit when we're away together. He's amazing with animals, isn't he?'

'Well – yes, I suppose he *is*!' said Mrs Layman. 'Although I can't say I like pet snakes, or pet beetles, and owls that come and hoot down the chimney at night to find out if Wilfrid will go out and hoot back at them!'

Julian laughed. 'We won't mind that,' he said. 'And he's managed to get over what might have been our biggest difficulty – he's made friends with our dog, Timmy. In fact, he informed us that if Timmy stayed, we could *all* stay – but *only* if Timmy stayed!'

Mrs Layman laughed. 'That's so like Wilfrid,'

she said. 'He's an odd boy. Don't stand any nonsense from him!'

'We won't,' said Julian, cheerfully. 'I'm surprised he wants to stay on with us, actually. I'd have thought he'd rather go home than be with a lot of strangers.'

'He can't go home,' said Mrs Layman. 'His sister has measles, and his mum doesn't want Wilfrid to catch it. So you'll have to put up with him, I'm afraid.'

'And he'll have to put up with us!' said Julian. 'Thanks very much for letting us have the cottage, Mrs Layman. We'll take great care of everything.'

'I know you will,' said the old lady. 'Well, goodbye, Julian. Have a good time. I'll get back to my car now. Give Wilfrid my love. I hope he doesn't fill the cottage with animals of all kinds!'

'We won't mind if he does!' said Julian, and waited politely until Mrs Layman had disappeared and he could hear the noise of a car starting up.

He went back to the cottage and stood outside, looking down at the amazing view. The harbour was full of boats, big and little. A boat went busily along, making for a great seaside town far away on the other side.

Anne came to join Julian. 'Glorious, isn't it?' she said. 'We're so very high up here that it seems as if we can see half the world at our feet. Is that an island in the middle of the harbour, Ju?'

'Yes – and a well-wooded one too!' said Julian. 'I wonder what it's called – and who lives there. I can't see a single house there, can you?'

Dick called to Anne. 'Anne! George and I are going to fetch our bikes and ride down to the village. Give us your shopping list, will you? Julian, is there anything special you want us to pack for you at home, and bring back, besides your night things and a change of clothes?'

'Yes – don't go off yet!' called Julian, hurrying into the cottage. 'I've made a list somewhere. I think I'd better go with you. There'll be food and other things to bring back – unless Mum would bring everything up by car this afternoon.'

'Yes – that's a good idea,' said Dick. 'We'll go to Kirrin Cottage first and get George's things – and then home to get ours. I'll leave all the shopping with Mum, and all our luggage, so that she can pop up here in the car with it. She'll love the view!'

'I'll stay behind and tidy up the cottage, and find out how the stove works,' said Anne, happily. 'I'll have everything neat and tidy by the time Mum comes this afternoon, Dick. Oh, here's Julian with the list. Why don't you go off on your bike with George and Dick, Julian? I'll be quite happy here messing about.'

'Yes, I'm going to,' said Julian, putting his list into his pocket. 'Look after yourself, Anne! We'll take Timmy with us, to give him a run.'

Off went the three, Timmy loping behind, very glad of the run. Anne waited till they were out of sight, then went happily back to the cottage. She was almost there when she heard someone calling her. She turned and saw a fresh-faced woman waving.

'I'm Sally!' she called. 'Do you want any help with the cooking and cleaning? Wilfrid told me not to come any more, but if you want me, I will.'

'Oh, I think we can manage, Sally,' said Anne. 'There's so many of us now, we can all do the jobs. Did you sleep here?'

'Oh no!' said Sally, coming up. 'I just came in to help, and then went back home. You tell me if you want me any time, and I'll gladly come. Where's that monkey of a Wilfrid? He spoke to me very rudely this morning, the little devil! I'll tell his grandmother of him – not that that's much good! He just laughs at her! Don't you stand any nonsense from him!'

'I won't,' said Anne, smiling. 'Where do you live, in case we *do* want you?'

'Just the other side of the road, in the small wood there,' said Sally. 'You'll see my tiny cottage when you go by the wood on your bikes.'

She disappeared up the hill and across the road there. Anne went back happily to her household tasks. She cleaned out the little larder, and then found a bucket and went to the well. She hung the bucket on the hook at the end of the rope, and then worked the old handle that let the bucket down to the water, swinging on the rope. Splash! It was soon full, and Anne wound it up again. The water looked crystal clear, and was as cold as ice – but all the same Anne wondered if she ought to boil it.

Someone came quietly behind her – and jumped at her with a loud howl! Anne dropped the bucket of water, and gave a scream. Then she saw it was

Wilfrid, dancing round her, grinning.

'Idiot!' she said. 'Now you just go and get me some more water.'

'Where's that big dog?' demanded Wilfrid, looking all round. 'I can't see him. You can't stay here unless you have that dog. I like him. He's a wonderful dog.'

'He's gone down to the village with the others,' said Anne. 'Now will you please pick up that bucket and get more water?'

'No, I won't,' said Wilfrid. 'I'm not your servant! Get it yourself!'

'All right, I will. But I'll tell George, who owns Timmy, how rude you are – and you can be *quite* sure that Timmy won't be friends with you,' said Anne, picking up the bucket.

'I'll get the water, I'll get the water!' shouted Wilfrid, and snatched the bucket. 'Don't you dare to tell George or Timmy tales of me. Don't you dare!'

And off he went to the well and filled the bucket. Well! What a time they were all going to have with such a very strange boy! Anne didn't like him at all!

5 Wilfrid is very annoying –
and Anne is very surprising!

Wilfrid brought back the bucket to Anne, and dumped it down.

'Like to see my pet beetles?' he said.

'No thank you,' said Anne. 'I don't like beetles very much.'

'Well, you ought to!' said Wilfrid. 'I've got two very beautiful ones. You can hold them if you like. The tiny feet feel very funny when they walk all over your hand.'

'I don't *mind* beetles, but I don't want them walking over my hand,' said poor Anne, who really was a bit afraid of what she called 'creepy-crawly' things. 'Please get out of my way, Wilfrid. If you had any manners, you'd carry that bucket indoors for me.'

'I *don't* have any manners,' said Wilfrid. 'Everybody tells me that. Anyway, I don't want to carry your bucket if you don't want to see my beetles.'

'Oh, go away!' said Anne, exasperated, picking up the bucket herself.

Wilfrid went to a little thick bush and sat down by it. He put his face almost on the grass, and looked under the bush. Anne felt uncomfortable. Was he going to call his beetles out? She couldn't help putting down her bucket, and standing still to watch.

No beetles came out from under the bush – but something else did. A very large, awkward-looking toad came crawling out, and sat there, looking up at Wilfrid with the greatest friendliness. Anne was amazed. How did Wilfrid know the toad was there? And why on earth should it come out to see *him*? She stood and stared – and shivered, because she really did *not* like toads.

'I know they have beautiful eyes, and are intelligent, and eat all kinds of harmful insects, but I just can't go near one!' she thought. 'Oh – Wilfrid's tickling its back – and it's scratching where he's tickled – just like we would!'

'Come and say hello to my pet toad,' called Wilfrid. 'I'll carry your bucket for you then.'

Anne picked up her bucket in a hurry, afraid that Wilfrid might whistle up a few snakes next. What a boy! How she wished the others would come back! Wilfrid might own a boa constrictor – or have a small crocodile somewhere – or ... but no, she was being silly! If *only* the others would come back!

To her horror the toad crawled right on to Wilfrid's hands, and looked up at him out of its really beautiful eyes. That was too much for Anne. She fled into the cottage, spilling half the water as she went.

'I wish I was like George,' she thought. 'She wouldn't mind that toad. I'm silly. I ought to try and like *all* creatures. Oh no, look at that enormous spider in the corner of the sink! It's sitting there, looking at me out of its eight eyes!'

'Wilfrid, Wilfrid – PLEASE come and get this spider out of the sink for me!'

Wilfrid sauntered in, fortunately without the toad. He held his hand out to the spider and made a strange clicking, ticking noise. The spider perked up at once, waved two curious little antennae about, and crawled across the sink to Wilfrid's hand. Anne shuddered. She simply couldn't help it! She shut her eyes and when she opened them, the spider had gone and so had Wilfrid.

'I suppose he's now teaching it to dance, or something,' she thought, trying to make herself smile. 'I can't *think* how insects and animals and birds like him. I just can't *bear* him. If *I* were a rabbit or a bird or beetle, I'd run miles away from him. What's this strange attraction he has for creatures of all kinds?'

Wilfrid had completely disappeared, and Anne thankfully went on with her little jobs. 'I'll tidy up the loft where the boys will sleep,' she thought. 'I'll wash this living room floor. I'll make a list of the things in the larder. I'll clean that dirty window over there. I'll . . . oh, what's that noise?'

It was the sound of magpies chattering noisily – a harsh but pleasant noise. Anne peered out of the little cottage window. Well, what a sight! There stood Wilfrid in front of the window, a magpie on each outstretched hand – and one on the top of his head! It stood there, chattering loudly, and then turned round and round, getting its feet mixed up in the boy's thick hair.

'Come out here and I'll tell one of my magpies to sit on your head too!' shouted Wilfrid. 'It's such a nice feeling. Or would you like a young rabbit to cuddle? I can call one for you with my little pipe!'

'I don't *want* a magpie on my head,' said Anne, desperately. 'For goodness' sake get a nice little baby rabbit. I'd like that.'

Wilfrid jerked the magpies off his hands and shook his head violently so that the third one flew up, squawking cheerfully. He then sat down and pulled out his funny little whistle-pipe, as Anne called it. She watched, fascinated, as the strange little dirge-like tune came to her ears. She found her feet walking to the door. Could there be some strange kind of magic in that pipe that made *her* go to Wilfrid, just as the other creatures did?

She stopped at the door, just as a baby rabbit came lolloping round a tall clump of grass. It was the funniest, roundest, sweetest little thing, with a tiny bobtail and big ears.

It went straight to Wilfrid and nestled against him. The boy stroked it and murmured to it. Then he called to Anne softly.

'Well – here's the baby rabbit you asked for. Like to come and stroke it?'

Anne went softly over the grass, expecting the

rabbit to bolt at once. Wilfrid continued to stroke it, and the little thing looked at him with big, unwinking eyes. Anne bent down to stroke it – but immediately it leapt in fright and fled into the grass.

'Oh *no* – why did it do that?' said Anne, disappointed. 'It was all right with you! Wilfrid, how do you get all these creatures to come to you?'

'Not telling you,' said Wilfrid, getting up. 'Is there anything to eat in the cottage? I'm hungry.'

He pushed Anne aside and went into the cottage. He opened the larder door, and took down a tin. There was a cake inside and he cut off a huge piece. He didn't offer Anne any.

'Couldn't you have cut *me* a piece too?' said Anne. 'You really are a rude boy!'

'I *like* being rude,' said Wilfrid, munching his cake. 'Especially to people who come to my cottage when I don't want them.'

'Oh, don't be so *silly*!' said Anne, exasperated. 'It *isn't* your cottage – it belongs to your grandmother. She told us so. Anyway, you said we could stay if Timmy stayed too.'

'I'll soon make Timmy *my* dog,' said Wilfrid,

another bite. 'You'll see! Soon he won't want that girl George any more – and he'll follow at my heels all day and night. *You'll* see!'

Anne laughed scornfully. Timmy following at this boy's heels? That could never happen! Timmy loved George with all his doggy heart. He would never desert her for Wilfrid, no matter how much he whistled on pipes, or put on his special croony voice. Anne was absolutely certain of that!

'If you laugh at me, I'll call up my grass snake *and* my adder!' said Wilfrid, fiercely. 'Then you'll run for miles!'

'Oh no I won't!' said Anne, hurrying into the cottage. 'Just watch *yourself* run!'

She picked up the bucket of water, went out with it, and threw it all over the astonished Wilfrid! Somebody else was *very* astonished too – and that was Julian, who had arrived back before the others, anxious not to leave Anne alone in the cottage for too long.

He came just in time to see Anne drenching Wilfrid, and stared in the utmost amazement. *Anne* behaving like that? Anne looking really *fierce* – quiet, peaceful Anne! What on earth had happened?

'Anne!' he called. 'What's the matter? What's Wilfrid been doing?'

'Oh – *Julian*!' said Anne, glad to see him, but horrified that he had come just then.

Wilfrid was drenched from head to foot. He stood there, gasping, taken aback, bewildered. Anne had seemed such a *quiet*, frightened little thing – scared even of a spider!

'That girl!' said Wilfrid, half choking, shaking the water off himself. 'That bad, wicked girl! She's like a tiger! She sprang at me, and threw the water all over me! I won't let her stay in my cottage!'

The boy was so angry, so wet, so taken aback, that Julian had to laugh! He roared in delight, and patted Anne on the back. 'The mouse has turned into a tiger! Well, you said you might one day, Anne – and you haven't lost much time! Let me see if you've grown claws!'

He took Anne's hands and pretended to examine her nails. Anne was half laughing, half crying now, and pulled her hand away. 'Oh Julian, I shouldn't have soaked Wilfrid – but he was so IRRITATING I lost my temper, and—'

'All right, all right – it's quite a good thing to

do sometimes,' said Julian. 'And I bet young Wilfrid deserved all he got. I only hope the water was icy cold! Do you have a change of clothes here, Wilfrid? Go and get into them, then.'

The boy stood there, dripping wet, and made no effort to obey. Julian spoke again. 'You heard what I said, Wilfrid. Hurry up! Go and change!'

The boy looked so wet and miserable that Anne felt suddenly sorry for what she had done. She ran to him and felt his wet shoulders.

'Oh, I'm *sorry*!' she said. 'Truly I am. I don't know *why* I turned into a tiger so suddenly!'

Wilfrid gave a little half laugh, half sob. 'I'm sorry too,' he mumbled. 'You're nice – and your nose is like that baby rabbit's – it's – it's a bit woffly!'

He ran into the cottage and slammed the door.

'Let him be for a while,' said Julian, seeing that Anne made a move to go after him. 'This'll do him good. Nothing like having a bucket of cold water flung over you to make you see things as they really are! He was really touched when you said you were sorry. *He's* probably never apologised to anyone in his life!'

'*Is* my nose like a rabbit's?' said Anne, worried.

'Well, yes – just a bit,' said Julian, giving his sister an affectionate pat. 'But a rabbit's nose is very nice, you know – very nice indeed. I don't think you'll have much trouble with Wilfrid after this little episode. He didn't know that you had the heart of a tiger, as well as a nose like a rabbit's!'

Wilfrid came out of the cottage in about ten minutes, dressed in dry clothes, carrying his wet ones in a bundle.

'I'll hang those out on the bushes for you, to dry in the sun,' said Anne, and took them from him, smiling.

He suddenly smiled back.

'Thanks,' he said. 'I don't know how they got so wet! Must have been *pouring* with rain!'

Julian chuckled and patted him gently on the back.

'Rain can do an awful lot of good at times!' he said. 'Well, Anne, we've brought you back a whole lot of goods for your larder. Here come the others. We'll carry everything in for you – with Wilfrid's help too!'

6 Lucas – and his tale

It was fun storing all the shopping away. Anne enjoyed it more than anyone, for she really was a very domesticated person.

'A real home-maker!' said Dick, appreciatively, when he saw how neat and comfortable she had made the loft, where the three boys were to sleep. 'Just about room for the three of us, plus all the baggage in the corner! And how good the larder looks!'

Anne looked at her well-stocked larder, and smiled. Now she could give her little 'family' really nice meals. All those tins! She read the names on them. Fruit salad. Tinned pears. Tinned peaches. Sardines. Ham. Tuna. A new cake in that round tin, big enough to last for at least three days. Biscuits. Chocolate wafers – good old Julian – he knew how much she loved those – and George did, too!

Anne felt very happy as she arranged all her

goods. She no longer felt guilty at drenching poor Wilfrid. Indeed she couldn't help feeling a little thrill when she remembered how she had suddenly turned into a tiger for a minute or two! It was fun to be a tiger for once.

'I might even be one again, if the chance arose,' thought Anne. 'HOW surprised Wilfrid was – and Julian too. Oh dear – poor Wilfrid. Still, he's much nicer now.'

And indeed he was! He was very polite to them all, and, as Dick said, he didn't 'throw his weight about' nearly so much. They all settled down very well together in the little cottage.

They had most of their meals outdoors, sitting on the warm grass. It was rather a squeeze indoors, for the cottage really was very small. Anne enjoyed herself preparing the meals, with sometimes a little help from George – and the boys carried everything out. Wilfrid did his share, and was pleased when he had a pat on the back from Julian.

It was glorious sitting out in the sun, high up on their hill. They could look down on the harbour, watch the yachts and the busy little boats, and enjoy the wonderful views all around.

George was very curious about the island that lay in the middle of the harbour.

'What's it called?' she asked Wilfrid.

But he didn't know. He did know, however, that there was a strange story about it.

'It belonged to a rich but lonely old man,' he said. 'He lived in a big house in the very middle of the wood. The island was given to his family by a king – James the Second, I think. This old man was the very, very last one of his family. People kept wanting to buy his island, and he had some kind of watchmen to keep people from landing on it. These watchmen were pretty fierce – they had guns.'

'Did they shoot people who tried to land, then?' asked Dick.

'Well – they just shot to frighten them off, not to hurt them, I suppose,' said Wilfrid. 'Anyway, a lot of sightseers had a terrible fright when they tried to land. BANG-BANG! Shooting all round them! My granny told me that someone she knew, who had a lot of money, wanted to buy part of the island – and *he* had his hat shot right off when his boat tried to land!'

'Is there anyone there now?' asked Julian. 'I

suppose the old man's dead? Did he have a son or anyone to follow him?'

'I don't think so,' said Wilfrid. 'But I don't know an awful lot about it. I'll tell you who does, though – one of the groundsmen on the golf course, called Lucas. He was once one of the watchmen who kept visitors away from the island.'

'It might be interesting to talk to him,' said Dick. 'I'd like to walk over the golf course, too. My dad plays golf, and I know a bit about it.'

'Well, let's go now,' said George. 'Timmy is longing for a good long walk, even though he ran all the way down to the village and back yesterday! Walk, Timmy? Walk?'

'Woof-woof,' said Timmy, and leapt up at once. Walk? Of *course* he was ready for a walk! He leapt all round George, pretending to pounce at her feet. Wilfrid tried to catch hold of him, but couldn't.

'I wish you were *my* dog,' he told Timmy. 'I'd never let you out of my sight.'

Timmy ran up to him then, and gave him a loving lick. It was astonishing how he seemed to like Wilfrid. Nobody could understand it.

As George said, 'Timmy's usually so particular about making friends! Still, Wilfrid *is* nicer than he was!'

The Five, with Wilfrid too, went up the hill, crossed over the road that ran along the top, and climbed over a stile. They found themselves on one of the fairways of the golf course not far from a green, in which stood a pole with a bright-red flag waving at the top.

Wilfrid knew very little about the game of golf, but the others had watched their parents play many a time.

'Look out – someone's going to pitch his ball on this green,' said Julian, and they stood by the hedge to watch the man play his ball.

He struck it beautifully with his club, and the ball rose, and fell right on to the green. It rolled very close to the hole in which the flagpole stood.

Timmy ran forward a few steps, as he always did when a ball rolled near him. Then he remembered that this was golf, and he must never, never touch a ball on the fairway or on the green.

The players passed, and went on with their

game. Then they disappeared, to play off another tee.

'Well, let's see if we can find Lucas now,' said Wilfrid, crossing the fairway to where he could get a good look over the course. 'You'll like him. There's not much he doesn't know about the animals and birds here. *I* think he's a wonderful man!'

Wilfrid stood on the slope of a hill and looked all round.

'There he is!' he said, pointing to where a man was trimming up a ditch. 'See? Down there. He's using his billhook to make things tidy.'

They went down the hill towards the ditch at the bottom.

'I bet there's an awful lot of balls in that ditch,' said Wilfrid. 'Hey, Lucas! How are you?'

'Morning, young man,' said the groundsman, turning towards them. His face was as brown as a well-ripened nut, and his arms and shoulders were even browner. He wore no shirt or vest, and his dark, deep-set eyes twinkled as they took in the five children and the dog.

He held out a brown hand to Timmy, who licked it gravely, wagging his tail. Then Timmy smelt Lucas all over and finally lay down with his head on the man's feet.

'Ha!' said Lucas to Timmy, and gave a loud, hearty laugh. 'Think I'm going to stand here all morning, do you? Well, I'm not. I've got work to do, old dog, so get up! You're a right good-un, you are, lying on my foot so I can't move a step! Want me to stop and have a rest, don't you?'

'Lucas, we came to ask you something,' said Wilfrid. 'About the island in the harbour. What's its name – and does anyone live there now?'

'We can see it from that little cottage almost at the top of the hill on the other side of the road,' said Dick. 'It looks very quiet and lonely.'

'And so it is,' said Lucas, sitting down on the bank of the ditch.

Timmy at once sat up beside him, sniffing him with pleasure. He put his arm round the dog, and began to talk, his bright eyes going from one to another of the children. He was so friendly, and so completely natural, that the children felt he was an old, old friend. They sat down too, sniffing the smell of the gorse bushes nearby.

'They smell like coconut,' thought Anne. 'Yes – just like coconut!'

'Well, now,' said Lucas, 'that island's always been a mystery place. It's called Wailing Island by some folks because the wind makes a right strange wailing noise round some of its high cliffs. And others call it Whispering Island because it's full of trees that whisper in the strong winds that always blow across it. But most of us call it Keep-Away Island – and that's the best name of all, for there's never been any welcome there, what with the dark cliffs, the cruel rocks, and the dense woods.'

Lucas paused, and looked at the listening faces around him. He was a born storyteller, and knew it. How often Wilfrid had listened to his tales of the birds and animals he met during his work on the course! Lucas was one of the few people that the boy admired and loved.

'Do go on, Lucas!' said Wilfrid, touching the man's bare, warm arm. 'Tell us about the old man who lived on the island years ago.'

'I'm telling the story my own way,' said Lucas, with great dignity. 'Be patient now, or I'll start my ditching again. Sit like this dog, see – he doesn't even twitch a muscle, good dog that he is. Well now, about this old man. He was so afraid of being robbed that he built himself a great castle right in the middle of the thick woods. Cut down about a hundred trees to make room for it, so the story goes, and brought every single stick and stone from the mainland. Did you see the old quarry on this here golf course, as you came along to me?'

'Yes, we did,' said Julian, remembering. 'I felt sorry for anyone who sent a golf ball there!'

'Well, out of that quarry came the great stones that the old man used for his castle,' said Lucas. ''Tis said that big, flat-bottomed boats had to be made to ferry the stones across to the island – and to this day the road through this golf course is the one made by horses dragging the great stones down to the water's edge.'

'Were you alive then?' said Wilfrid.

'Bless you, boy, no, of course not,' said Lucas, with a great chuckle of a laugh. 'Long before my time, that was. Well, the stone house – or castle, whatever you like to call it – was built. And the old man brought to it all kinds of treasures – beautiful statues, some of gold, it was said, but I don't believe that. There are many strange tales I've heard of what that rich old man took over to

Whispering Island – a great bed made of pure gold, and set with precious stones – a necklace of rubies as big as pigeons' eggs – a wonderful sword with a jewelled handle, worth a king's fortune – and other things I can't remember.'

He paused and looked round. Julian asked him a quick question. 'What happened to all these things?'

'Well now, he fell foul of the king of the land, and one morning, what did he see landing on the shores of his island but ships of all kinds,' said Lucas, enjoying the rapt attention of his audience. 'A lot of them were sunk by the wicked rocks but enough men were left to storm the strange stone castle in the wood, and they killed the old man and all his servants.'

'Did they find the treasures the old man had collected?' asked Dick.

'Not one thing!' said Lucas. 'Not one thing. Some say it was all a tale – the old man never did bring any wonders there – and some say they're still there, on Whispering Island. I think it's all a yarn – but a good yarn at that!'

'Who owns the island now?' asked Dick.

'Well, an old man and his wife went to live

there – maybe they paid rent to the Crown for it, maybe they bought it – but they didn't care for anything except for the birds and the animals there,' said Lucas, picking up his curved billhook again, and hacking lightly at some briars. 'They wouldn't allow anybody there, and it was they who kept the gamekeepers with guns to frighten away sightseers. They wanted peace and quiet for themselves, and for all the wildlife on the island – and a good idea too. Many a time when I was there with the other keepers – three of us there were – many a time I've had rabbits gambolling over my feet, and snakes gliding by me – and the birds as tame as canaries.'

'I'd *love* to go there,' said Wilfrid, his eyes shining. 'I'd have a good time with all the wild creatures! Can anyone go there now?'

'No,' said Lucas, getting up. 'Not a soul has lived in the old stone castle since the old man and his wife fell ill and died. The place is empty. The island belongs to a great-nephew of the old couple now, but he never goes there. Just keeps a couple of men on the island to frighten off visitors – pretty fierce they are, so I've been told. Well, there you are, that's the story of Whispering Island –

not very pleasant – a bit grim and ugly. It belongs to the birds and the beasts now, and good luck to them!'

'Thank you for telling us the story,' said Anne, and the old countryman smiled down at her, his eyes wrinkling, and his brown hand patting her cheek.

'I'll be off to my hedging and ditching again,' he said, 'and I'll feel the sun warm on my bare back, and hear the birds singing to me from the bushes. That's happiness enough for anyone – and it's a pity that more folks don't know it!'

7 Up on the golf course

The children walked round the golf course together, after talking to old Lucas.

'We must keep out of the way of anyone playing,' said Dick, 'or we might get hit on the head with a ball! Hey, Timmy, what are you doing in the bracken?'

Timmy came out with something in his mouth. He dropped it at George's feet. It was a golf ball, fairly new. George picked it up.

'What do we do with this?' she said. 'There's no golfer near us. It must be a lost ball.'

'Well, all balls lost on golf courses should be taken in to the pro,' said Julian. 'By right they belong to him if found on the course.'

'What's a pro?' asked Anne.

'A professional golfer – someone who's very, very good at the game, and is in charge of a golf course,' explained Julian. 'Hey look! Here comes Tim again with *another* ball. Timmy, we ought to

hire you out to golfers who keep losing their balls
– you'd save them no end of trouble!'

Timmy was pleased to be patted and praised.
He set off into the rough again at once, sniffing
here and there.

'Anyone would think that golf balls smelt like
rabbits or something, the way Timmy sniffs
them out!' said Anne, as Timmy ran up with yet
another ball. 'Golfers must be really careless,
losing so many balls!'

They went on round the course, which was set
with great stretches of gorse, full of brilliant
blossom. A baby rabbit fled from the bracken as
Timmy nosed there for balls. Timmy chased it,
and the frightened little creature dodged this way
and that, trying to escape.

'Let it go, Tim, let it go!' yelled George,
but Timmy was much too excited to pay
any attention.

Wilfrid suddenly bent down as the rabbit
raced near him, and gave a strange low whistle.
The rabbit swerved, came straight towards him,
and leapt into his arms, lying there trembling.
Timmy jumped up to it at once, but George
dragged him away.

'NO, Timmy. Sorry, but NO, you can't have the little thing. Down! DOWN, I say!'

Timmy gave George a disgusted look. He was very cross with George. Rabbits were meant to be chased, weren't they? Why did George have to spoil his fun?

George stared at Wilfrid. The rabbit was still nestling in his arms, and he was making a strange noise to it. The tiny thing was trembling from head to tail. Everyone watched it, glad that it was safe. They were all silent, astonished at the way that Wilfrid had rescued the little creature. How had the rabbit known that Wilfrid's arms were ready to save it?

He took it to the bracken, dropped it gently, and watched it race like lightning to the nearest burrow. Then he turned and patted Timmy, who stood silently by, watching.

'Sorry, Tim,' he said. 'It's so little, and you're so big!'

'Woof,' said Tim, exactly as if he understood, and he gave Wilfrid's hand a quick lick. Then he pranced round the boy, barking, as if he wanted a game, and Wilfrid raced off with him at top speed.

The others followed, impressed once again by Wilfrid's uncanny way with animals. He was such a horrible boy in some ways – so rude, so mannerless, so selfish – then how was it that animals liked him so much? George frowned. She thought it was all wrong that animals should love Wilfrid and go to him – even Timmy was all over him! If she wasn't careful he'd spend more time with Wilfrid than with her! That would never do!

Timmy found five more balls, and soon Julian's pockets were heavy with them. They made their way to the small clubhouse in the distance, meaning to give in the balls. It was set in a little dip, and looked friendly and welcoming. They all went in at the door, and Julian walked over to the pro, who was checking some scorecards. He emptied his pockets of balls and grinned.

'A present from our dog!' he said.

'Did he find all those?' said the pro, pleased. 'Not bad ones, either. I'll buy you all some lemonade or orangeade – which will you have?'

They all had orangeade, and the pro sent a packet of biscuits to Timmy, who was waiting patiently outside. He was delighted!

'We're staying in that little cottage up on the hillside,' said Dick. 'Do you know it?'

''Course I do!' said the pro. 'My grandmother lived there once upon a time. You've got a wonderful view there, haven't you? One of the best in the world, I reckon! You can see Whispering Island from there, too. Ought to be called Mystery Island! It's said that people have gone there and never come back!'

'What happened to them?' asked Anne.

'Oh well – maybe it's all a tale!' said the pro. 'There's supposed to be priceless things there, packed away somewhere – and collectors from all over the world have come here, and tried to get over to that island – not to steal, you understand, but just to see if they could find anything worthwhile and buy it for museums – or maybe for their own collections. It's said there are statues in the wood, white as snow – but that I never did believe!'

'And didn't the collectors ever come back?' asked Julian.

'It's said that a lot of them didn't,' said the pro, 'but that may all be silly tales. But I do know that two men came down here from some museum in London, and hired a boat to go across. They took a white flag with them so that the two keepers wouldn't shoot them – and after that nobody heard a word about them. They just disappeared!'

'Well – what could have happened to them?' asked Julian.

'Nobody knows,' said the pro. 'Their boat was found miles out to sea, drifting – and empty. So the police reckoned a mist came down, they lost direction, and ended by drifting way out to sea.'

'But did they jump out of their boat, and try to swim back – and get drowned?' asked Dick. 'Or did a passing ship or yacht save them?'

'They weren't picked up, that's certain,' said the pro. 'Else they'd have arrived safely back at their homes, sometime or other. But they didn't. No – I reckon the poor men were drowned. Of course, maybe they were shot by the keepers, when they tried to land, and their boat was set adrift!'

'Didn't the police do anything?' asked Julian, puzzled.

'Oh, yes – they went across to the island in the coastguard patrol boat,' said the pro. 'But the keepers swore they'd seen nobody arriving, and that they were the only people on the place. The police landed and searched everywhere, and they found nothing except the great white castle-like house in the woods and hundreds of wild animals, so tame that they'd sit and watch you as you walked by.'

'All very mysterious,' said Julian, getting up. 'Well, thanks for the orangeade, and for your information! We'd already heard a bit from a groundsman of yours – Lucas – a real countryman, and a born storyteller!'

'Ah, Lucas – yes, he knows that island well,' said the pro. 'He was once one of the keepers, I believe! Well – come and see me again some time – thanks for the balls. It isn't everyone who's honest enough to come and give them in when they find them!'

They all said goodbye and went out. Timmy pranced along in joy. Sitting down outside the clubhouse didn't suit him at all!

'Did you enjoy your biscuits, Tim?' asked George, and he ran up and gave her hand a quick lick. What a question! He *always* enjoyed biscuits! He ran off into the bracken and began to nose about there again, hunting for balls.

The others went to walk up the hill, talking about the island.

'I wonder what really *did* happen to those two collector men who were never heard of again,' said Anne. 'Funny that their boat was found adrift and empty.'

'They must have been drowned, of course,' said Dick. 'I wonder if anything *is* left of the old treasures that were once taken there. No – there wouldn't be – the police would have made a very thorough search!'

'I wish *we* could go to the island!' said George. 'I don't expect the keepers would shoot at *us*, would they? They might even let us on, to make a change for them – they must be so bored with only themselves to talk to.'

'That's *very* wishful thinking, George,' said Julian. 'We're DEFINITELY not going near the island, so put that right out of your head.'

'Well – I knew it was impossible, really,' said George. 'But wouldn't it be a *wonderful* adventure if we managed to get on the mysterious Whispering Island and explore it without the keepers knowing!'

'Not such a wonderful adventure if we were all peppered with shot from the keepers' guns!' said Dick. 'Anyway, we wouldn't find anything of interest – the treasures must have been removed long ago. The only possible things of interest would be the very tame wild creatures there! Wilfrid would go mad with joy – wouldn't you, Wilfrid?'

'I'd like it very much,' said the boy, his eyes shining. 'What's more, I might hire a boat myself and row round the island to see if I could spot any animals there.'

'You'll do nothing of the sort!' said Julian, at once. 'So don't try any silly tricks, OK?'

'I won't promise! said Wilfrid, irritatingly. 'You just never know!'

'Oh yes, I do know! You're just trying to sound big!' said Julian. 'Come on quickly, everyone – it's past our dinner-time, and I'm ravenous! What's for lunch, Anne?'

'We'll open a tin of tuna,' said Anne, 'and there's plenty of bread left, and lettuce, which I left in water. And tomatoes. And lots of fruit.'

'Sounds good!' said George. 'Dinner, Timmy, dinner!'

And, hearing that welcome word, Timmy shot up the steep hill at top speed, his tail waving joyously.

'Wish I was a dog and could run up a hill like that!' said Anne, panting. 'Give me a push, Julian! I'll *never* get to the top!'

8 *Mostly about Wilfrid*

Timmy was waiting for the children at the top of the hill, his tail waving, his mouth open as he panted. He picked something up, as the children came, threw it into the air, and caught it.

'Another golf ball, Timmy?' said Dick, as Timmy threw the ball into the air again with a toss of his big head.

'No – it's too big for that,' said George. 'Drop it, Timmy. What have you found?'

Timmy dropped the ball at George's feet. It was bigger than a golf ball, and had a hole right through it.

'Oh, it's one of those balls that children throw up and try to catch on a stick,' said George. 'Somebody must have dropped it. All right, Tim, you can have it.'

'He won't swallow it, will he?' said Wilfrid, anxiously. 'It's not *very* big – and I once saw a dog swallow something by mistake, that he threw into the air to catch.'

'Timmy's *much* too sensible to swallow *any* ball,' said George. 'You needn't worry about *him*. Anyway, *I* can do any worrying necessary. He's *my* dog.'

'All right, all right, all right!' said Wilfrid. 'Miss High-and-Mighty can look after her own dog. Fine!'

George looked round at him furiously and he made a face at her. Then he whistled to Timmy – yes, he actually dared to whistle to him!

'Nobody whistles for my dog except me,' said George. 'And anyway, he won't come to *you*.'

But, to her surprise and horror, Timmy *did* go to Wilfrid, and pranced all round him, expecting a game. George called him sternly, and he looked at her in surprise. He began to trot over to her when Wilfrid whistled again, and obediently Timmy turned as if to go to him.

George caught hold of the dog's collar, and aimed a punch at the whistling boy. It missed him, and he danced round, laughing.

'Stop it now, you two,' said Julian, seeing George's look of fury. 'I said STOP IT! Wilfrid, go on ahead, and *keep* going. George, don't be an idiot. He's only teasing you to make you lose your temper. Don't please him by losing it!'

George said nothing more, but her eyes blazed.

'Oh dear!' thought Anne, 'now we won't have any peace! She won't forgive Wilfrid for making Timmy go to him! Wilfrid really is a pain sometimes.'

They were all very hungry for their lunch and very pleased with everything that Anne provided. Dick went into the little cottage to help her. George insisted on keeping her hand on Timmy's collar all the time, in case Wilfrid should entice him to his side.

'He's making some of his strange noises now,' said Dick to Anne. 'Noises that animals can't seem to resist! I'm not surprised that George has got Timmy tightly by the collar! I'm not a dog, but I find those little whiny noises Wilfrid is making very strange indeed, and I'd love to go nearer!'

'Well, I hope we're not going to have black looks from George from now on,' said Anne. 'Wilfrid's an idiot at times, and VERY irritating – but he's not bad underneath, if you know what I mean.'

'Well, I don't really,' said Dick, cutting some tomatoes in half. 'I think he's a badly brought-up little pain – and if I were a dog, I'd bite him, not fawn on him! Have I cut up enough tomatoes, Anne?'

'Oh yes!' said Anne. 'How many do you think we're going to eat – forty or fifty? Look, you open this tin for me, Dick. I hate opening tins. I nearly always cut myself.'

'Don't you ever open one again, then,' said Dick. 'I'm the official tin opener from now on! Anne, what would we do without you? You take everything on your shoulders, and we just *let* you! We all ought to help you more.'

'No, don't,' said Anne, in alarm. 'I *like* doing things on my own. You lot would only break things or knock them over. You're all so clumsy when it comes to washing up or setting out crockery, although I know you *mean* well.'

'So we're all clumsy, are we?' said Dick, pretending to be offended. 'When have *I* ever broken anything, I'd like to know? I'm just as careful as you when I handle crockery!'

Poor Dick! The glass he was holding suddenly slipped from his hand, fell to the floor, and broke!

Anne looked at him and gave a sudden delighted giggle. 'Clumsy!' she said. 'Can't pick up a glass without dropping it! Look, take out this tray for me, and for goodness' sake don't drop *that*!'

They all had a delicious lunch, and ate practically everything. Wilfrid sat a little away from everyone, scattering crumbs around as he ate. Birds of all kinds were soon around him, even hopping on to his hands. A magpie flew down to his left shoulder. Wilfrid greeted it like an old friend. 'Hello, Maggie Pie! How's the family? I hope Polly Pie has recovered from her cold. And is Peter Pie's bad leg better? And what about old Grandpa Pie – does he still chase you young ones?'

The magpie put its glossy head on one side and chattered back to him in bird language, which Wilfrid appeared to understand. He stroked the bird's gleaming breast. George deliberately didn't watch. She turned her back on Wilfrid and the magpie, and talked to Timmy. The others couldn't help being amused.

The magpie put an end to Wilfrid's conversation very suddenly. The boy was about to put half a tomato into his mouth when the bird bent down its head and snatched away the tomato with its powerful beak. Then it rose quickly into the air on its big wings, making a noise exactly as if it were laughing!

Everyone roared with laughter except the surprised Wilfrid.

'He's gone to take your tomato to Polly Pie, I should think,' said Anne, and that made everyone laugh again.

'I'll have another tomato now, please,' said Wilfrid.

'Sorry. You're unlucky. They're all gone,' said Dick.

It was lovely sitting up on the hillside, watching the boats in the harbour, and seeing the beautiful, white-sailed yachts bending to and fro in the strong wind that blew there. They could all see Whispering Island quite clearly, and noticed that no boats went anywhere near it. Clearly everyone knew that men might be there, watching for intruders.

'There might be badgers there,' said Wilfrid, suddenly. 'I've never been really *close* to a badger.'

'I shouldn't think anyone but you would *want*

to be!' said George. 'Smelly things! There's one thing – you can't call one with your whistle-pipe – there aren't any here!'

'Wilfrid – get out your pipe and make the little rabbits come again,' said Anne, suddenly. 'While we're all sitting here quietly. Would they come?'

'Yes, I think so,' said Wilfrid, and felt in his pocket. He felt in another pocket, and looked worried. Then he stood up and patted himself all over, looking really distressed. He stared round at the others, anguish on his face.

'It's gone,' he said. 'I must have lost it! It's gone and I'll never have another one like it, never.'

'Oh, it *must* be in one of your pockets,' said Dick, touched by the look on the boy's face. 'Here, let *me* feel.'

But no – the pipe wasn't there. Wilfrid looked as if he were about to burst into tears. He began to hunt all around, and everyone helped him. No – not quite everyone. George didn't. Dick glanced at her, and frowned. George was *pleased* that the precious pipe was lost. How she must dislike poor Wilfrid! Well, he was dislikeable at times, no doubt about it – but he was so distressed now that surely nobody could help feeling sorry for him!

George got up and began to clear away the remains of the meal. She carried plates and glasses to the cottage, and after a while Anne followed her.

'I'm sorry for poor old Wilfrid, aren't you?' she said.

'No, I'm not,' said George, shortly. 'Serves him right! I hope he never finds his silly pipe. That'll teach him not to try and get Timmy away from me!'

'Oh, don't be silly! He only does it for fun!' said Anne, shocked. 'Why do you take things so seriously, George? You know Timmy loves you better than anyone in the world and always will. He's your dog and nobody, nobody else's! Wilfrid's only teasing you when he tries to get Timmy to go to him.'

'Timmy goes, though,' said George, desperately. 'And he shouldn't. He *shouldn't.*'

'He can't help it, I think,' said Anne. 'Wilfrid has some strange attraction for animals – and that little whistle-pipe of his is like a magic call to them.'

'I'm *glad* it's gone!' said George. 'Glad, glad, glad!'

'Then I think you're silly and unkind,' said Anne, and walked off, knowing that she could do nothing with George in this mood.

She worried a little as she went. Did George *know* where the pipe was? Had *she* found it – and hidden it – or destroyed it? No – no! George could be difficult and unkind at times, but she wasn't *mean*. And *what* a mean thing it would be, to destroy the beautiful little pipe with its magic trills!

Anne went back to the others, meaning to try and comfort Wilfrid – but he wasn't there.

'Where's he gone?' asked Anne.

'To look for his precious whistle-pipe,' said Dick. 'He's really heartbroken about it, I think. He says he's going to walk back the way we came from the golf course, and then he's going to walk everywhere there that we walked this morning, and hunt and hunt. He's even going down to the clubhouse to see if he dropped it there. He'll never find it!'

'Poor old Wilfrid!' said Anne, tender-hearted as ever. 'I wish he'd waited for me. I'd have gone with him. He's very upset, isn't he? Won't he be able to call the wild animals to him any more?'

'I've no idea,' said Dick. 'Er – I suppose George doesn't know anything about it? Perhaps that's a mean thing to say – but George might have found it and kept it just for a joke.'

'No. No, I don't think she'd do that,' said Anne. 'It'd be a *very* bad joke. Well – we'll just have to hope Wilfrid finds it. What are you going to do this afternoon? Sleep, by the look of you!'

'Yes – sleep out in the warm sun here, till three o'clock,' said Julian. 'Then I'm going for a walk – down to the harbour. I might even have a swim.'

'We'll all go,' said Dick, sleepily. 'Oh how lovely it is to feel lazy – and warm – and well fed – and sleeeeeeepy! See you later, everyone! I'm asleep!'

9 *Off to Whispering Island*

The two boys, and Anne and George, slept soundly in the sun until just past three o'clock. Then a large fly buzzed around Anne's head and awoke her. She sat up and looked at her watch.

'Oh! It's ten past three!' she said, in surprise. 'Wake up, Julian! Dick, stir yourself! Don't you want to go and swim?'

Yawning loudly the two boys sat up and looked all round. George was still asleep. Wilfrid hadn't yet come back.

'Still hunting for his precious pipe, I suppose,' said Anne. 'Get up, you two boys. Dick, *don't* lie down, you'll only go to sleep again. Where are your swimming things? I'll get them. And does anyone know where our swimming towels are? We'll probably have to dress and undress with them round us!'

'They're up in our room, chucked into a corner,' said Dick, sleepily. 'Oh, I *was* sound asleep. I really thought I was in my bed when I woke up!'

Anne went to fetch the swimming towels and the swimming things. She called back to the boys. 'I've got everything. Come on, Julian, *don't* go to sleep again!'

'Right!' said Julian, sitting up and stretching himself. 'Oh, this sun – it's GLORIOUS!'

He poked Dick with his toe. 'Get up! We'll leave you behind if you snore again. George, goodbye – we're going!'

George sat up, yawning, and Timmy stood over her and licked her cheek. She patted him. 'All right, Timmy, I'm ready. It's so warm that I'm LONGING for a dip – and you'll love it too, Tim!'

Carrying their swimming things they made their way down the hill, and across a stretch of moorland to the edge of the sea, Timmy running joyously behind them. Beyond lay Whispering Island, a great tree-clad mass, and all around and about little boats plied, and yachts sailed in the wind, enjoying themselves in the great harbour which stretched far beyond the island to a big seaside town on the opposite coast.

The four went behind some rocks, and stripped off their clothes, emerging three minutes later in their scanty swimming things. Anne raced to the edge of the water, and let it lap over her toes.

'Lovely!' she said. 'It's not a bit cold! I'll enjoy my swim!'

'Woof!' said Timmy and plunged into the water.

He loved the sea too, and was a good swimmer! He waited for George to come in and then swam to her. She put her arms round his neck and let him drag her along with him. 'Dear Timmy! How strong he is,' thought George.

They had a wonderful time in the water. Further out the waves were big and curled over like miniature waterfalls, sweeping the children along with them. They yelled in joy, and choked when the water splashed into their mouths. It was an ideal day for swimming.

When they came out, they lay on the sand in the sun, Timmy beside George, keeping guard as usual. It was really warm. George sat up and looked longingly out to sea, where the wind was whipping up the waves tremendously.

'Wish we had a boat!' she said. 'If we were back home, I could get out my own boat, and we could go out in the cool breeze and get dry.'

Julian pointed lazily to a big notice not far off. It said 'BOATS FOR HIRE. ENQUIRE AT HUT.'

'Oh good!' said George. 'I'll go and ask. I'd *love* a good row!'

She slipped on her sandals, and went to the hut to which the sign pointed. A boy of about fifteen sat there, staring out to sea. He looked round as George came along.

'Want a boat?' he said.

'Yes, please. How much?' asked George. 'For four of us – and a dog.'

'Better to take it by the week if you're staying here,' said the boy. 'It works out very cheap then.'

George went back to the boys and Anne.

'Shall we take the boat by the week?' she said. 'We could do lots of rowing about, and it'd be fun.'

'Right,' said Dick. 'Anyone got any money?'

'There's some in my pocket, but not enough, I'm afraid,' said Julian. 'I'll go and arrange for us to have the boat tomorrow – we'll take it for a whole week. I can easily bring the money with me in the morning.'

The boat boy was very obliging. 'You can have

the boat today and onwards, if you like, you needn't wait till tomorrow,' he said. '*I* know you'll bring me the money all right! So, if you'd like to have it this afternoon, it's up to you. Choose which boat you like. They're all the same. If you want to take it out at night too and do some fishing, you can – but tie it up safe, won't you?'

'Of course,' said Julian, going to look at the boats. He beckoned to the others, and they all came over.

'Any boat we like, day *or* night!' said Julian. 'Which do you fancy? *Starfish – Splasho – Adventure – Seagull – Rock-a-bye*? They all look good, sound little boats to me!'

'I'd like *Adventure*, I think,' said George, thinking that that particular little boat looked sturdy, clean and sound. 'Nice name – and nice little boat!'

So *Adventure* it was!

'And a really good name for any boat of ours!' said Dick, pushing it down to the sea with Julian. 'Whooooosh! There she goes! Steady – we want to get in! Chuck in all the clothes, George! We can dress when we feel cold.'

Soon they were all in the boat, bobbing about

on the waves. Julian took the oars and pulled out
to sea. Now they were in the full breeze – and a
strong one it was too!

'I'm certainly not hot any more!' said
George, pulling her swimming towel round
her shoulders.

The tide was running out, and pulled the boat
strongly out to sea. Whispering Island suddenly
seemed very much nearer!

'Better look out!' said George, suddenly.
'We don't know if a keeper's on guard somewhere
on the shore of the island. We're getting
pretty near.'

But the outgoing tide swept the boat on and on
towards the island, so that very soon they could
see a sandy shore. Dick then took one oar, and
Julian the other, and they tried to row against the
tide and take the boat back into calm water.

It was no good. The tide was far too strong.
Very soon the boat was quite near the shore of
the island, and then an enormous wave flung
them right up the sand and left the boat grounded
as it went back again. It slid over to one side, and
they all promptly fell out!

'Whew!' said Julian. 'What a tide! I had no idea

it was so strong, or I'd never have brought the boat out so far.'

'What shall we do!' said Anne, rather scared.

She kept looking all around for a keeper with a gun. What if they got into real trouble through coming right on to the island?

'I think we'll have to stay on the island till the tide turns, and we can row back on it,' said Julian. 'I can't think why that boat boy didn't warn us about the tide. I suppose he thought we knew.'

They pulled the boat a little further up on the firm sand, took out their bundles of clothes and hid them under a bush. They walked up the beach towards a wood, thick with great trees. As they neared them, they heard a strange, mysterious sound.

'Whispering!' said George, stopping. 'The trees are *really* whispering. Listen! It's just as if they were talking to one another under their breath! No wonder it's called Whispering Island!'

'I don't like it much,' said Anne. 'It almost sounds as if they're saying nasty things about us!'

'Shooey, shooey, shooey, shooey!' said the trees, nodding towards one another as the wind shook them. 'Shooey, shooey!'

'JUST the noise of whispering!' said George. 'Well – what do we do now? We'll have to wait an hour or two till the tide turns again!'

'Shall we explore?' said Dick. 'After all, we've got Timmy with us. No one's likely to attack us if they see *him*!'

'They can shoot him, can't they, if they have guns?' said George. 'If he growled one of his terrifying growls, and ran at them showing his teeth, they'd be scared to bits and fire at him.'

'I think you're right,' said Julian, angry with himself for landing them all into what might be serious trouble. 'Keep your hand on Timmy's collar, George.'

'You know what I think?' said Dick suddenly. 'I think we ought to try and find the guards, and tell them the tide swept us on to the island by accident – we couldn't stop the boat surging on! We're not grown-ups, come to snoop around, so they're sure to believe us – and we'd be safe from any chasing or shooting then.'

They all looked at Julian. He nodded. 'Yes – good idea. Give ourselves up, and ask for help! After all, we hadn't any real intention of actually *landing* – the tide just *threw* the boat into that sandy cove!'

So they walked up to the back of the cove and into the wood, whose whispering was very loud indeed, once they were actually among the trees. No one was to be seen. The wood was so thick that it was in parts quite difficult to clamber through. After about ten minutes' very hard walking and clambering, Julian came to a stop. He had seen something through the trees.

The others pressed behind him. Julian pointed in front, and the others saw what looked liked a great grey wall, made of stone.

'The old castle, I imagine!' Julian whispered, and at once the trees themselves seemed to whisper even more loudly! They all made their way to the wall, and walked alongside it. It was a very high wall indeed, and they could hardly *see* the top! They came to a corner and peeped round. A great courtyard lay there – quite empty.

'Better shout, I think,' said Dick, beginning to feel rather creepy, but before they could do that two enormous men suddenly came down a flight of great stone steps. They looked so fierce that Timmy couldn't help giving a blood-curdling growl. They stopped short at once and looked all round, startled.

'The noise came from over there,' said one of the men, pointing to his left – and, to the children's great relief, both swung off in the wrong direction!

'We'd better get back to the cove,' whispered Julian. 'I don't like the look of those men at all – they look like real thugs. Quiet as you can, now. George, don't let Timmy bark.'

They made their way back beside the stone wall, through the whispering trees, and there they were at the cove.

'We'd better row back as quickly as we can,' said Julian. 'I think something's wrong here. Those men didn't look like gamekeepers. I wish we hadn't come.'

'Ju – where's our boat?' said Dick in a shocked voice. 'It's gone. This can't be the right cove!'

The others stared round. Certainly there was no boat! They *must* have come to the wrong cove.

'It looks the same cove to *me*,' said George. 'Except that the sea has come in a bit more. Do you think it took our boat away – look at that big wave sweeping right in – and sucking back!'

'Oh, yes! Our boat could easily have been dragged out on a wave like that!' said Julian, very worried. 'Look out – here comes another!'

'It *is* the same cove!' said Anne, looking under a bush at the back. 'Here are our clothes, look! We hid them here!'

'Take them out quickly!' called Julian, as another big wave swept right in. 'What an idiot I am! We should have pulled our boat as far up as we could.'

'I'm cold now,' said Anne. 'I'm going to dress. It'll be easier to carry a swimming costume than a heap of clothes!'

'Good idea!' said Dick, and they all promptly dressed, feeling warmer at once.

'We might as well leave our swimming things under the bush where we left our clothes,' said George. 'At least we'll know it's the same cove if we find them there!'

'The thing is – what are we going to do *now*?' said Julian, worried. 'No boat to get back in – and why on earth did we choose one called *Adventure*? We might have *known* something would happen!'

10 *The Five are in trouble*

Julian went to the mouth of the cove and looked out over the waves, hoping that he might see their boat bobbing somewhere. 'I could swim out to it if so,' he thought, 'and bring it in. No – there's not a sign of a boat! I could kick myself for being so careless!'

Dick came up, looking worried.

'I suppose it's too far to swim back to the mainland, isn't it?' he said. 'I could have a go – and get another boat and come back for everyone.'

'No. Too far,' said Julian. 'The tide's too strong for any swimmer at the moment. We're certainly in trouble.'

'We can't signal, I suppose?' said Dick.

'What with?' asked Julian. 'You could wave a shirt for an hour and it wouldn't be seen from the mainland!'

'Well – we have to think of *something*!' said

Dick, exasperated. 'What about trying to find a boat *here*? Surely those men must have one to get to and fro.'

'Of course!' said Julian, patting Dick on the back. 'Where are my brains? They seem to be going soft or something! We could snoop around and about tonight, to see if there's a boat anywhere. They may have two or three. They'd have to get food from the mainland at times.'

The two girls and Timmy came up then, and Timmy whined.

'He doesn't seem to like this island,' said George. 'I think he smells danger!'

'I bet he does!' said Dick, putting his hand on Timmy's firm head. 'I'm really glad he's with us. Can you girls think of any good ideas? We can't!'

'We could signal,' said George.

'No good. A signal from here couldn't be seen,' said Dick. 'We've already thought of that.'

'Well – if we lit a fire here on the beach tonight, when the tide's out, surely *that* would be seen?' said Anne.

Dick and Julian looked at one another.

'Yes!' said Julian. 'If we lit it on a hilly bit

it'd be better still – on that cliff up there, for instance.'

'Wouldn't the guards see it?' asked Dick.

'We'd have to chance that,' said Julian. 'Yes – we could do that. Good idea, Anne. But we're going to get really hungry, aren't we? Anyone got anything to eat?'

'I've got two bars of chocolate – a bit soft now though,' said George, digging into the pocket of her shorts.

'And I've got some peppermints,' said Anne. 'What about you boys? You always take barley sugars about with you, Dick – don't say you haven't any just when we could all do with them!'

'I've got a new packet!' said Dick. 'Let's all have one now!'

He pulled the packet from his pocket and handed it round. Soon they were all sucking barley sugars. Timmy was given one too, but his was gone in a flash!

'Wasted on you, Tim, absolutely *wasted*!' said Anne. 'Crick, crack, swallow – that's all a barley sugar means to you! Why can't dogs suck a sweet like we do! They never seem to suck *anything*.

No, Timmy, don't go sniffing into Dick's pocket for another!'

Timmy was disappointed. He went snuffling round the cove, and then, scenting a rabbit smell, he followed it with his nose to the ground. The children didn't notice that he had disappeared but went on talking, trying to solve their very real difficulty.

No boat. No food. No way of getting help except by signalling in some way. *Not* very funny, thought Dick.

And then, very suddenly, a loud sound broke the silence – CRACK!

Everyone jumped up at once.

'That was a gunshot,' said Dick. 'The keepers! But what are they shooting at?'

'Where's Timmy?' cried George, looking all round. 'Tim, Tim, where are you TIM?'

Everyone's heart went cold. Timmy! No, the shot couldn't have been meant for Timmy! Surely the keepers wouldn't shoot a *dog*!

George was nearly mad with dread. She clutched at Dick, tears streaming down her cheeks. 'Dick! It couldn't be Timmy, could it? Oh Timmy, where are you? TIMMY! Come to me!'

'Listen! Listen a minute, George!' said Dick, as shouts came from the distance. 'I thought I heard Tim whine then. Isn't that him coming through the bushes?'

There was the noise of rustling as some creature pressed through the last year's bracken fronds – and then Timmy's head appeared, his bright eyes looking for them.

'Oh Timmy, darling Timmy, I thought you'd been shot!' cried George, hugging the big dog. '*Did* they shoot at you? Are you hurt anywhere?'

'I bet I know why he was shot at,' said Dick. 'Look what he's got in his mouth – half a ham! Drop it, you robber, you!'

Timmy stood there, the ham in his mouth, wagging his tail joyously. He had felt hungry, and was sure the others did too – so he had gone hunting!

'Where did you get that, you bad dog?' said Julian.

Timmy wished he could tell him. He would have said, 'Well, I went sniffing after a rabbit – and I came to a shed stored with tins of food – and one was open with this piece of ham inside, waiting for me. And here it is!'

He dropped the ham at George's feet. It smelt extremely good.

'Well, thanks, boy,' said Julian. 'We could do with some of that – although we'll have to pay for it when we meet the owner, whoever he is!'

'Julian – he *has* been shot at!' said George, in a trembling voice. 'Look – his tail's bleeding, and some fur is gone.'

'Oh, yes!' said Julian, examining Timmy's tail. 'Those men mean business. I really think I'd better find them and tell them we're here, in case they take a potshot at us too!'

'Well, let's go *now* – all of us,' said Dick. 'They probably thought Timmy was a wolf or a fox or something, slinking through the trees. Poor old dog!'

Timmy wasn't at all disturbed. He was so proud of finding and bringing back the ham that he even wagged his wounded tail!

'No animals or birds will be tame and friendly on this island now,' said Anne. 'They'll have been scared stiff by the gamekeepers shooting at this and that.'

'You're right,' said Julian. 'It makes me think that the men on the island aren't just gamekeepers, put in to preserve the wildlife, and to frighten sightseers away – but real, fierce guards of some kind. Like those two horrible men we saw in the courtyard!'

'Well, what *are* they guarding then?' said George.

'That's what I'd very much like to find out,' said Julian. 'And I think perhaps I'll snoop around a bit and see what I can discover. When it's getting dark, though, not now.'

'I wish we hadn't come,' said Anne. 'I wish we were safe in our cottage with Wilfrid. I wonder if he's found his whistle-pipe. It seems *ages* since we hired that boat!'

'Can't we go quietly through the woods and explore a bit?' asked George. 'Or walk round the shore to see if there's a boat anywhere? I'm getting bored, sitting here, talking.'

'Well – I suppose Tim would give us warning at once if he heard anyone near,' said Julian, who was also longing to stretch his legs. 'We'll go in single file and make as little noise as we can. Timmy can go ahead. He'll give us instant warning if we come near any of the keepers.'

They all stood up, and Timmy looked at them, wagging his nicked tail. 'I'll look after you,' said his two bright eyes. 'Don't be afraid!'

They made their way carefully and quietly through the whispering trees. 'Sh, sh, sh, shoo, shooey,' said the leaves above their heads, as if warning everyone to go as quietly as possible. And then suddenly Timmy stopped and gave a low, warning growl. They all stood still at once, listening.

They could hear nothing. They were in a dense part of the wood, and it was dark and sunless. What was Timmy growling at? He took a step forward, and growled softly again.

Julian went forward too, as silently as he could. He stopped suddenly and stared. What on earth was that strange figure, gleaming out of the shadows? His heart began to beat loudly. The figure stood there, silently, an arm outstretched as if pointing at something!

He thought it moved and he took a step backwards in fear. Was it a ghost or something? It was so very, very white and shone so strangely. The others, coming up behind, suddenly saw it too and stopped in fright. Timmy growled again, and all the hackles on his neck rose up. What was this?

Everyone stood absolutely still, and Anne gave a gulp. She took hold of Dick's arm, and he held it tightly against him. And then George gave a very small laugh. To everyone's horror she went forward, and touched the hand of the gleaming figure.

'Hello,' she said. 'It's so nice to meet a well-mannered statue!'

Well! A statue! Only a *statue*! It had looked so real standing there, and yet so ghostly. Everyone heaved a sigh of relief, and Timmy ran forward and sniffed at the statue's flowing robes.

'Look around you,' said Julian. 'The wood's full of statues just here – and aren't they BEAUTIFUL! I hope they don't suddenly come alive – they really look as if they might!'

11 A strange discovery

The children were astonished to see so many gleaming statues standing in the darkness of the wood. They wandered round them, and then came to a large shed. They peeped inside.

'Look here!' said Dick, excited. 'Long, deep boxes, strong as iron! And see what's in these two!'

They all came to look. In the first, packed in what looked like sawdust, was a beautifully carved statue of a boy. The next box seemed to be entirely full of sawdust, and Anne had to scrape quite a lot away to see if anything was packed there too.

'It's a little stone angel!' she said, scraping sawdust from a quaint little face, a small crown and the tips of small wings. 'Lovely! Why are these statues being packed away like this?'

'Use your brain!' said Dick. 'It's obvious that they're works of art – and are probably very old.

They're being packed to send away in some boat or ship – to be transported somewhere where they'll fetch a lot of money – America, probably!'

'Did they come from the old castle, do you think?' asked George. 'It's quite near. I expect this shed belongs to it. But how was it that the police didn't find them in the castle when they searched? They must have gone there, and looked into every corner! And what about the statues in the wood outside – why haven't *they* been packed away?'

'Too big, probably,' said Julian. 'And too heavy. A small boat wouldn't be strong enough to take great things like that. But those little statues are perfect for transporting – they don't weigh as much as the big ones – and they aren't marked by the weather, through standing in rain, sun and snow! Not a mark on them!'

'You're right,' said Anne. 'I noticed that those big ones outside were green here and there, and some had bits knocked off them. I wish we could get inside the castle and see the things there!'

'The man at the golf club, the one we took those lost balls to – *he* said something about statues as white as snow, standing in this wood – do you remember?' said Dick.

'Yes. They must have stood there for some time,' said Julian. 'I don't think they can be very valuable, else they'd be put carefully indoors, under cover. But these little ones – I guess they're worth a lot of money!'

'Who do you think packed them in here?' said Anne.

'Maybe those big men we saw,' said Julian. 'Even small statues like these need someone very strong indeed to carry them here to this shed, and pack them like this. Then, of course, they'd have to be carried to some boat – or ship – probably to a boat first and then rowed out to a waiting ship. But I don't think those guards are the men behind all this – someone with a great knowledge of old things must be the ringleader. He probably heard the old legend of the island, came to have a look around, and made quite a lot of interesting discoveries!'

'*Where*?' asked George. 'In the castle?'

'Probably – although carefully hidden away!' said Julian. 'For all we know there may be lots of really valuable old treasures hidden there still.

That sword with a jewelled handle, for instance! And the bed made of gold, and—'

'To think they might all be quite near us, somewhere on Whispering Island!' said Anne. 'I'd love to be able to say I'd slept on a bed of pure gold!'

'Well, I think you'd find it very hard,' said Dick.

Timmy suddenly gave a small whine, and licked George's hand.

'What is it?' she said. 'What do you want, Timmy?'

'Perhaps he's hungry,' said Anne.

'Thirsty, more likely!' said Julian. 'Look at his tongue hanging out!'

'Oh, *poor* Tim – you haven't had a drink for hours!' said George. 'Well – where on earth can we get you one? We'll have to look for a puddle, I'm afraid. Come on!'

They left the shed where the beautiful little statues were lying in their sawdust, and went out into the sunshine. Everywhere was dry, Julian felt worried.

'We'll *all* be thirsty soon!' he said. 'I wonder where we can get some water?'

'Would it be too dangerous to go near the castle and see if there's a tap anywhere?' asked George, ready to face almost anything to get her dog a drink!

'Yes, it would,' said Julian, in a very decided voice. 'We're not going near any of those men with guns. They might have been told to shoot on sight, and that wouldn't be very pleasant. We'd be peppered all over with shot!'

'Look – what's that round thing over there – like a little circular wall?' said Dick, pointing to something behind the shed where the statues lay in their boxes.

They all went over to it – and Anne guessed what it was at once!

'A well! An old well!' she said. 'Look, it has an old wooden beam over the top, with a pulley to wind and unwind a bucket. *Is* there a bucket – let's hope so! We can let it down to the water and fill it for Timmy then.'

Timmy put his paws on the rim of the wall and sniffed. Water! That was what he wanted more than anything. He began to whine.

'All right, Timmy – we'll send the bucket down,' said George. 'It's still on the hook! Julian, this handle's really stiff – can you turn it to let down the bucket?'

Julian tried with all his strength – and quite suddenly the rope loosened, and the bucket gave a sudden jerk and jump. It jumped right off the hook, and with a weird echoing, jangling sound, fell from the top to the bottom of the well – landing in the water with a huge splash!

'No, no, no!' said Julian, and Timmy gave an anguished howl. He peered down at the lost bucket, now on its side in the water at the bottom of the well gradually filling itself.

'It'll probably sink below the water now,' said Julian with a groan. 'Is there a ladder down the well? – if so I could shin down and get the bucket.'

But there wasn't, although it looked as if there had been at some time, for here and there were staples in the brick side of the well wall.

'What can we do?' asked Anne. 'Can we possibly pull up the bucket?'

'No – I'm afraid we can't,' said Dick. 'But wait a minute – I could shin down the rope, couldn't I, and pick the bucket out of the water? And easily get up again, because George and Julian could turn the well handle, and pull me up that way!'

'Righto. Down you go then,' said Julian. 'The rope's good and strong, not frayed or rotten. We'll wind you and the bucket up all right!'

The boy sat on the side of the well wall, and reached out for the rope. He swung himself on to it, and swayed there a moment or two, looking down the long, dark hole below him, with the water at the bottom. Then down he went, hand-over-hand, just as he often did at school in the gym.

He came to the bottom, reached down, took hold of the bucket handle, and filled the bucket full. The water felt as cold as ice to his hand.

'All right. Pull me up!' he shouted, his voice sounding very hollow and strange as it rose up through the well walls.

Dick was heavy to pull up. Julian and George turned the handle valiantly, but it was slow work. Gradually Dick came up nearer and nearer to the top. When he was halfway they heard him give an exclamation, and call out something; but they couldn't make out what it was and went on winding the groaning rope, slowly but surely.

They reached down and took the bucket from

Dick as soon as his head appeared at the top. Timmy fell on it with excited barks, and began to lap vigorously.

'Didn't you hear me yelling to you to stop when I was halfway up?' demanded Dick, still swinging on the rope. 'Don't let go of that handle. Hang on to it for a minute.'

'What's the excitement?' asked Julian, in surprise. '*Why* did you yell to us? We couldn't make out what you said.'

Dick swung himself to one side, caught hold of the well top and hauled himself up, so that he could sit on the well wall. 'I shouted because I suddenly saw something quite strange as I came up the well,' he said. 'And I wanted to stop and see what it was!'

'Well – what *was* it?' asked Julian.

'I don't quite know. It looked just like a little door! An iron door,' said Dick. 'Hey, don't let Timmy drink all that water – he'll be ill. We'll let the bucket down again in a minute and get some more for ourselves.'

'Go on about what you saw,' said George. 'How *could* there be a door in the side of a well going deep down into the earth?'

'Well, I tell you, there *was* one,' said Dick. 'Look, Timmy's gone and knocked over the bucket now! Let's send it down on the pulley to be filled again, and I'll go down on the rope again too. But when I come up and you hear me shout "Stop" just stop winding, OK?'

'Here's the bucket for the hook,' said Julian. 'I'll be careful not to jerk it off this time. Ready?'

Down went Dick and the bucket again – splash went the bucket and filled with water once more. Then up came Dick again, wound up by Julian and George as before. As soon as they heard him shout 'Stop', they stopped their winding and peered down.

They saw Dick peering hard at the side of the well wall, and pulling at it with his fingers. Then he shouted again. 'All right. Up we go!'

They hauled him up to the top, and he clambered off the rope, swung himself on to the well wall and sat there.

'Yes. It *is* some kind of opening in the well wall – it *is* a door – and it has a bolt this side to undo, but it was too stiff for my fingers. I'd have to go down and jiggle it about with my knife before I could loosen it.'

'A door in a well! But where on earth would it lead to?' said Julian, astonished.

'That's what we're going to find out!' grinned Dick, rather pleased with himself. 'Who'd put a door in the side of a well? *Some*body did – but WHY? Very cunning – and mysterious – and unguessable. I think I'll go straight down again and see if I can open that door – and discover what it leads to!'

'Oh DO, Dick do!' said George. 'If you don't, *I* will!'

'Hang on to the rope. Down I go again!' said Dick.

And down he went, much to Timmy's surprise. The others looked down anxiously. Could Dick open the well door? What would he find behind it? Quick, Dick, quick – everybody's waiting for you!

12 A great surprise –
and a shock for George

As soon as Dick shouted 'Stop', Julian and George hung on to the rope to stop it going down any further. Dick was swinging just opposite the strange door. He began to feel round it, and to jiggle it. It had no lock, apparently, but there was a bolt on his side. He tried to push back the bolt – and suddenly it came away from the door, and dropped down into the well. It had rusted so much that it could not even hold to the door, once it was handled!

The door felt loose, now the bolt was gone. Dick ran his hands round it, trying to loosen it further, and banged it with his fist. Rust fell off it, and Dick's hands were soon brown with the old, old rust.

He saw a little knob at the top of the door and gave it a tug. Ah – the door felt looser now. He ran his knife all round the edges, scraping away all the rust he could find. Then he managed to get his strongest knife blade in between the door edge and the well wall, and used it as a lever to force the door open.

It opened slowly and painfully, with creaks and groans. Dick pulled it back with difficulty and then peered through the hole.

He could see nothing at all but black darkness – how very disappointing! He fumbled in his pocket to see if he had a torch. Yes – good! He shone it through the little door, his hand trembling with excitement. What would he see?

His torch was small and not very powerful. The light fell first of all on a face with gleaming eyes, and Dick had such a shock that he almost fell down the well. The eyes seemed to glare up at him in a very threatening manner! He switched his torch to the right – and yet another face gleamed up to him.

'An odd face,' thought Dick. 'Yellow as can be! YELLOW! YELLOW! I think that face is made of gold!'

His hand trembling even more, he shone his torch here and there through the opening, catching first one yellow face in its light, and then another.

The faces had yellow bodies too, and their eyes glinted very strangely.

'I believe – I really do believe – that I've found the hiding place of the golden statues,' thought Dick. 'And those gleaming eyes must be precious jewels. I did have a shock when I saw them all looking at me! Whatever is this place they're in?'

'DICK! What can you see? Please tell us!' yelled Julian, and poor Dick almost fell off the rope when the shouts echoed round him.

'Pull me up!' he shouted. 'It's unbelievable! Pull me up and I'll tell you!'

And before a minute had passed he was standing by the others, his eyes gleaming almost as brightly as the eyes of the golden statues, his words tumbling over one another.

'That door leads into the place where all the treasures are hidden. The first thing I saw was a golden statue staring at me – brilliant eyes in a yellow face – a golden face, real gold! There are dozens of them. I don't think they liked me very much – they glared at me! They didn't say a word – although I half expected them to. What a hiding place – right down under the earth!'

'There must be another entrance to it,' said

Julian, thrilled to hear such extraordinary news. 'The well door must be a secret one. Statues couldn't be pushed through it. What a find, Dick.'

'Let's all go down in turn and look through the door!' said George. 'I can't believe it. I think I must be dreaming it. Quick, let me go down!'

One by one they all went down on the rope and looked through the door. Anne came back rather scared. She had felt very strange when she had seen the silent statues looking at her.

'I know they're not *really* looking, it's only that their eyes gleam,' she said. 'But I kept expecting one or other to take a step forward and speak to me!'

'Well – the next thing to do is to climb through the door, and see exactly where the statues are underground,' said Julian. 'And find out the opening *they* were brought in by. There must be a door the other end of their room, through which they were brought. What a hiding place, though! No wonder the police couldn't find any statues or other treasures.'

'We might find the golden sword there, with the jewelled handle!' said Anne. 'And the golden bed.'

She had hardly finished speaking when there came a loud noise from behind them. Timmy was barking his head off! Whatever was the matter?

'Shh!' said George, fiercely. 'You'll bring the guards here, you idiot! Stop it!'

Timmy stopped barking and whined instead. Then he ran off towards the wood, his tail waving happily.

'Who on earth is he going to meet?' said George, amazed. 'Someone he knows, by the look of his tail!'

The others all followed Timmy, who raced along towards the cove where they had landed – and lost their boat. And there, in the cove, was another boat! A small one, to be sure, but still a boat – and by it, stroking Timmy, was Wilfrid! Wilfrid! What an amazing thing!

'WILFRID! How did you get here – did you hire that boat? Did you come all by yourself? Did you . . .'

Wilfrid grinned round in delight, thrilled at the surprise he was giving everyone. Timmy licked him without stopping, and George didn't even seem to notice!

'Well,' he said, 'you didn't come back, so I

guessed something was wrong – and when the boat boy told me you'd taken one of his boats and it had been reported tossing about, empty, on the water near the island, I guessed what had happened – I said, "Aha! they didn't make the boat secure when they got to the island – and now they're marooned there!" You were pretty mean to go without me – but I guessed you'd be pleased to see me if I borrowed a boat and came over!'

Anne was so pleased that she gave the boy a hug.

'Now we can go back whenever we want to,' she said.

'But we *don't* want to, at the moment,' said Dick. 'We've made some amazing discoveries, Wilfrid – and I'm really pleased you'll be able to share in them! Er – what have you got in your pocket? Something keeps poking its head out at me.'

'Oh, that's only a baby hedgehog,' said Wilfrid, taking it out gently. 'It got trodden on – by a horse, I think – so I'm just caring for it for a day or two.' He put it back into his pocket. 'But go on – tell me what you've found. Not the lost treasures, surely?'

'Yes!' said Anne. 'We saw them when we went down a well near the castle.'

'Did somebody throw them into the water there?' said Wilfrid, amazed.

'No,' said Dick, and told him about the strange door in the side of the well wall.

Wilfrid's eyes nearly fell out of his head.

'I *am* glad I came!' he said. 'I nearly didn't. I thought you wouldn't really want me – and I knew George wouldn't be pleased, because of Timmy. I can't help him coming round me – and anyway he'd feel hurt if I pushed him off.'

Timmy came nosing round him at that moment, with his ball. He wanted Wilfrid to throw it for him. But Wilfrid didn't notice the ball. He just patted the soft head, and went on talking.

'The boat boy wasn't very pleased when he heard that the boat you hired was loose on the sea. He said you'd hired it for a week, and there it was, back the same day, wet and empty! His cousin brought it in. No damage done.'

'I'll make it up to him when I see him,' said Julian. 'I haven't paid him for the hire of it either, but he knows I will, when I get back. I had no idea that the sea would throw up waves that could drag out an unmoored boat.'

'You ought to have taken me with you,' said Wilfrid, grinning.

Timmy, tired of trying to make him throw his ball, went off to George, who was only too pleased to. She threw it into the air, and Timmy leapt up and caught it.

Then, very suddenly, he made a horrible noise and rolled over, kicking as if he were in great pain.

'What's the matter, Timmy?' cried George, and rushed to him.

Wilfrid ran too. The dog was choking, and his eyes were almost popping out of his head.

'That ball's stuck in his throat!' cried Wilfrid. 'I knew it was dangerous! I told you it was! Cough it up, Timmy, cough it up. Oh, you poor, choking thing! Oh Timmy, Timmy!'

The boy was beside himself with fear that the dog would choke, as he had once seen another dog do, and as for George, she was wild with terror. Poor Timmy's eyes looked terrible as he choked and choked, trying to get the ball out of his throat.

'He'll choke to death,' cried Wilfrid. 'Julian,

force his mouth open, and hold it. I must try to get out the ball. Quick!'

Timmy was growing weaker, and it wasn't too difficult to force his mouth wide open. Wilfrid could see the ball down the dog's throat – the ball with the hole in the middle. He put his small hand into the dog's big mouth, and forced his forefinger into the hole in the ball. His finger joint stuck there – Wilfrid gently drew back his hand – and the ball came too, on his finger! There it was, with his finger still stuck in the hole! Timmy began to breathe again, great panting breaths, while George stroked his head and cried for joy that he was all right.

'I shouldn't have given you that ball, I shouldn't!' she said. 'It was too small for a big dog like you – and you *will* throw them up in the air and catch them. Oh Timmy, Timmy, I'm very, very sorry. Timmy, are you all right?'

Wilfrid had gone off, but now came back with some water in the bucket. He dipped his hand in it and let drops of water drip into the dog's mouth. Timmy swallowed it gratefully. His throat was sore, but the water was cool and soothing. George let Wilfrid do this without a word. She looked rather white and shaken. Timmy might be dead by now if Wilfrid hadn't put his finger into that hole in the ball and drawn it out!

'Thank you, Wilfrid,' she said, in a low voice. 'You were very clever.'

'Thank goodness the ball had a hole through it,' said Wilfrid, and he put his arms round Timmy's neck. The dog licked him gratefully. Then he turned and licked George too.

'He says he belongs to both of us now,' said George. 'I'll share him with you. You saved his life.'

'Thanks,' said Wilfrid. 'I'd love to have just a *bit* of him – he's the nicest dog I know!'

13 A meal – a sleep – and a disappearance

'I feel hungry again,' said George, who always had a very good appetite indeed. 'We've finished all that ham, haven't we? I *had* to give Timmy some. What about a barley sugar, Dick?'

'Two more left for each of us – just ten,' said Dick, counting. 'Sorry, Timmy – none for you this time. Have one, everybody. We'll have five left then!'

'Oh, I forget to tell you,' said Wilfrid, taking a barley sugar. 'I brought some food in my boat! I didn't think you'd taken any, and I guessed you'd soon be really hungry!'

'You're wonderful, Wilfrid!' said Julian, wondering why he had ever disliked the boy. 'What have you brought?'

'Come and see,' said Wilfrid, and they all went over to the boat, Timmy walking as close to the boy as he could.

Higgledy-piggledy in the boat was a pile of tins, a large loaf of bread, and some butter, looking rather soft.

'Oh good!' said Anne, in delight. 'But how on earth did you carry all this from the cottage to your boat? Look, everyone, Wilfrid's even brought some plates and spoons!'

'I put everything into a sack, and carried it over my shoulder,' said Wilfrid, enjoying everyone's delighted surprise. 'I fell over going down the hill to the shore and all the tins rolled out, and *shot* down the slope!'

Everyone laughed at the thought of tins rolling at top speed down the hill. Anne slipped her arm through Wilfrid's and gave it a squeeze.

'You did really well,' she said and Wilfrid beamed at her, astonished and pleased at everyone's warm friendliness. Timmy went up to the boat and began sniffing at the bread. Then he turned and barked as if to say 'Is there anything here for *me*?'

Wilfrid understood at once.

'Oh *yes*, Timmy!' he said. 'I brought a special tin of dog food for you – here you are – a large tin of Waggomeat!'

Timmy recognised the tin at once, and barked joyfully. He pawed Wilfrid as if to say 'Come on, then – open it! I'm hungry!'

'Anyone got a tin opener?' said George. 'It'd be awful if we couldn't open the tins!'

'Oh – I never even *thought* about that!' said Wilfrid. 'What an idiot I am!'

'It's all right. I've got a thing on my penknife that's *supposed* to open tins,' said Dick, taking out a very large closed knife. 'I've never bothered to use it – so let's hope it *will* do the trick. Chuck me a tin, Wilfrid.'

Wilfrid threw him the tin of Waggomeat. With everyone watching very anxiously indeed, Dick opened a strange looking tool in his knife, and jabbed the point into the top of the tin. It worked!

'First time I've ever used it,' said Dick, running the gadget round the tin top. 'Three cheers for the person who thought of including it in a knife!'

'Will Timmy be able to swallow yet?' asked George, anxiously. 'His throat must still be hurting him where that wooden ball choked him.'

'Oh, Timmy will be able to judge that for himself,' said Julian. 'If I know anything about him not even a sore throat will stop him from wolfing half that tin!'

Julian was right. As soon as Dick scraped out a third of the meat with his knife on to a flat stone nearby, Timmy was wolfing it in great gulps!

'Nothing much the matter with your throat now, Tim!' said Anne, patting him. 'Dear Tim. Don't ever choke again. I couldn't bear it!'

'Let's have a meal ourselves now,' said George. 'We'll open more of those tins. We don't need to be stingy about them because we can leave in Wilfrid's boat at any time, and get back to the mainland.'

Soon they had opened a tin of tuna, two tins of fruit and a large tin of baked beans. They cut the big loaf into six pieces (one for Timmy, of course) and then sat down at the back of the cove to feast.

'Best meal I ever had in my life!' said Dick, enjoying himself. 'Tasty food – fresh air – sea nearby – sun on our heads – and friends sitting all round me!'

'Woof!' said Timmy, at once, and gave Dick a very wet lick.

'He says he couldn't agree more,' said Anne with a laugh.

'The sun's going down,' said George. 'What are we going to do? Go back to the mainland in Wilfrid's boat – or stay here for the night?'

'Stay here,' said Julian. 'Nobody knows we're here, and I want to snoop around a bit tonight, when those men can't see me. There's a lot of things that puzzle me. For instance, how on earth do they send away the things from here – like those packed statues we saw? It must mean that a fairly big vessel comes along to collect them, I suppose. And I'd like to know how many men there are on the island – presumably the guards we saw, with guns – and the men who've found that underground cave, where everything was hidden. Then we'll go back, tell the police, and leave things to them!'

'Perhaps the others should go back to the mainland now,' said Dick. 'I don't think we should all run the risk.'

Before Julian could reply, George spoke quickly – and crossly. 'We're staying here – although Anne can go back if she wants to. But Timmy and I are staying with you boys, so that's that.'

'All right, all right, no need to shout!' said Dick, pretending to cover his ears. 'What about you, though, Anne? You're the youngest, and . . .'

'I'm staying,' said Anne. 'I'd be worried stiff all night if I left you on the island. And I don't want to miss any excitement!'

'Right,' said Julian. 'We all stay then. Wilfrid, did you know that Timmy has his nose in the pocket where you keep your hedgehog?'

'Yes. They're just making friends,' said Wilfrid. 'Anyway, the hedgehog's only a baby – his quills won't prick Timmy's nose, they're still too soft. He's a sweet little thing. I thought I'd call him Spiky.'

'Wuff,' said Timmy, quite agreeing.

He was sitting between George and Wilfrid, very happy indeed, for both stroked him and patted him at the same time.

'I think I'll take a walk round the island,' Wilfrid announced suddenly. 'Timmy, like to come with me?'

Timmy got up at once, but George pulled him down. 'Don't be an idiot, Wilfrid,' she said. 'Timmy's been shot at once by the men here – and I'm not going to risk it again – besides, we don't want them to know we're here.'

'I'd be very careful,' persisted Wilfrid. 'I wouldn't let them spot me. They didn't spot me coming over in the boat.'

Julian sat up very suddenly. 'How do we know they didn't?' he said. 'I never thought of that! They might have a telescope – they might keep watch all the time – they might even have seen *us* in *our* boat! After all, they can't risk being spied on!'

'I don't *think* they could have seen us,' said Dick. 'They'd have made a search.'

'I'm sure they didn't see *me*,' boasted Wilfrid. 'They'd have been waiting for me on the shore, if they had.' He got up and looked all round. 'I think I'll go for my walk now,' he said.

'NO! You're DEFINITELY not going for a walk, Wilfrid,' said Julian, and lay back in the sun again. It was sinking now, but still very bright. Dick began to think of the night, and how he and Julian would snoop around and find the way into that strange place underground where those golden statues stood silently in the darkness.

Then he fell asleep, and only awoke when Anne gave him a friendly shove. He sat up and began a long and leisurely conversation with his sister – and then Anne suddenly looked all round.

'Where's Wilfrid?' she said. They *all* sat up then, and looked startled. Wilfrid was nowhere to be seen!

'He must have slipped away without a sound! said Dick, angrily. 'The little idiot. He's been gone ages! He'll get caught, for sure. Good thing Timmy didn't go with him – he might have been caught too – and shot!'

George put her arms round Timmy in fear.

'Timmy would never go with Wilfrid if I wasn't there too,' she said. 'What a little idiot he is! Those men will guess there's someone else on the island with Wilfrid, won't they? They might even *make* him tell all he knew – and where the boat is, and everything!'

'What shall we do?' said Anne. 'We'd better go after him.'

'Timmy'll track him for us,' said George, getting up. 'Come on, Tim. Find Wilfrid. Find that silly boy Wilfrid!'

Timmy understood at once. He put his nose to the ground, found Wilfrid's scent, and began to walk away.

'Not too fast, Timmy,' said George, and he at once slowed down. George looked round at the little place among the bushes where they had been sitting. 'Had we better take a tin or two with us?' she said.

'Yes. Good idea,' said Julian. 'You just never know!'

He and Dick took a couple of tins each, stuffed uncomfortably into their pockets. Stupid Wilfrid!

'He must have gone in this direction,' said Dick. 'I never spotted him slinking away, the little nuisance! I'm surprised Timmy didn't make a sound! Track him, Tim, track him!'

'Listen!' said Anne, suddenly, and she stopped. 'Listen!'

They all listened – and didn't at all like what they heard. It was Wilfrid's voice, yelling in fright.

'Let me go! Let me go!'

And then a stern, loud and threatening voice came. 'Who are you with? Where are they? You're not alone, we're certain of that!'

'Quick – we must hide!' said Julian, angry and worried. 'Dick, look about for a good place and I will too.'

'No good,' said Dick. 'They'll beat everywhere for us. Better climb trees.'

'Good idea!' said Julian. 'Anne, come with me. I'll give you a shove up. Hurry, everybody! Hurry!'

14 Wilfrid has an adventure on his own

'What about Timmy? He can't climb,' said George, fearfully. 'He might be shot.'

'Put him under a bush and tell him to sit, sit, sit!' said Julian, urgently. 'He knows what that means. Go on, George, quick.'

George took Timmy by the collar and led him to a very thick bush. She pushed him under it. He turned himself round, poked his nose out of the leaves, and looked at her in surprise.

'Sit, Timmy! Sit, and keep quiet!' said George. 'Sit, sit, sit – and keep *quiet*. Understand?'

'Woof,' said Timmy, very quietly, and withdrew his nose so that nothing of him could be seen at all. He knew perfectly well what George meant. Clever Timmy!

Dick was giving Anne a shove up a tree with drooping branches thick with leaves.

'Get as high as you can,' he said, in a low voice.

'And then stay put till you hear me call you. Don't be afraid. Timmy's down here to protect you!'

Anne gave him rather a small smile. She wasn't like George, fearless and always ready to rush into trouble. Anne was all for a peaceful life – but how could she have that if she was one of the Five?

The boys and George were now high up in trees, listening to the shouting going on. Apparently Wilfrid wasn't going to give away his friends – good for him!

'How did you get here?' a man was shouting.

'In a boat,' said Wilfrid.

'Who was with you?' shouted another man.

'Nobody. I came alone,' said Wilfrid, perfectly truthfully. 'I wanted to visit the island. I'm an animal lover and I heard that all the wild creatures here were tame.'

'A likely story that!' sneered a man's voice. 'Huh! Animal lover!'

'All right then – look what I've got here in my pocket,' said Wilfrid, and apparently showed the man his baby hedgehog. 'He was trodden on by a horse – and I've been looking after him.'

'Very well – you can go back to your boat, and

row away,' said the man. 'AT ONCE, mind. And don't look so scared. We won't hurt you. We've business of our own here, and we don't want strangers around – not even silly little kids with hedgehogs in their pockets!'

Wilfrid took to his heels and fled. He felt lost now. He would never find the others – or the cove where his boat was. WHY had he disobeyed Julian? Had the others heard the men shouting at him? Which way should he go?

He had entirely lost his sense of direction and had no idea whether to go to the left or the right. He began to panic. Where could the others be? He *must* find them, he must! He ran through the trees, wishing that Timmy was with him. Then he stopped. Surely this was quite the wrong way? He turned and went in a different direction. No, this couldn't be right either, he didn't recognise a thing!

He thought he heard voices in the distance. He stood and listened. Could it be the others? If only George would tell Timmy to find him! But she wouldn't, in case he was shot at. *Was* that noise voices – or was it just the wind? Perhaps it was the others looking for him. Wilfrid rushed off towards the distant sound. But it died down. It was only the wind!

The trees thinned out in bushes – and then Wilfrid suddenly saw the sea in the distance! Good! If he could get to it, he could walk round the shore till he came to his cove. He would know where he was then. He began to run towards the blue sea.

Through the bushes he went, and came out at last on to what seemed to be a very high cliff. Yes – there was the sea, below and beyond. If only he could scramble down the cliff he could bear to the right and at last come to his cove. He came to the edge of the cliff and looked down – and then he started back in fear. What was that noise – that awful, dreadful noise? It was like a giant wailing and wailing at the top of his voice, the wailing going up and down in the wind. Wilfrid found his knees were shaking. He simply didn't dare to go on. He sat down and tried to get his breath, putting his hands over his ears to keep out the horrible wailing.

And then he suddenly remembered something and heaved a sigh of heartfelt relief. 'Of course – these must be the Wailing Cliffs we were told about,' he thought thankfully. 'We heard about the Whispering Wood – and it *does* whisper – and the Wailing Cliffs – and they *do* wail! At least, it's really the wind, of course. But what a strange sound!'

He sat for a while longer, then, feeling much bolder, he went to the edge of the great cliff, and looked over. He stared down in surprise.

'There's somebody down there – three or four people! Mustn't let them see me – they must belong to the men on the island! What are they doing down there?'

He lay down and peered over. Four men were there – but, as Wilfrid watched, they disappeared. Where had they gone? He craned over the cliff to see. 'There must be caves in the cliff, I suppose,' he said to himself. 'That's where they've gone! Oh, I wish this wailing would stop. I'll start wailing myself in a minute!'

After some time voices came faintly up to him, as he lay watching, and he saw two men coming out on to the rocks below again. What were they carrying? A long, deep box – it looked exactly like one of the boxes in which the others had seen those beautiful little statues, packed in sawdust!

'So *that*'s how they get them away from here – take them down through some passage in the cliffs to a waiting boat. Where's the boat, though? I can't see one. Not arrived yet, perhaps.'

He watched with intense interest as the men carried out box after box and piled them on a great flat rock that abutted a stretch of fairly calm water.

'Big boxes – little ones – those men have been busy lately!' thought Wilfrid, wishing and wishing and wishing that the others were with him. 'I wonder what's in them. Not the bed of gold, that's certain. I bet it'd be far too big to put into a boat. Have to be pulled to pieces first! Oh – here comes another box – a small one this time. Wow, they'll soon need a ship to take all these!'

Almost as he thought it, he saw a small boat in the far distance! 'Well! There's the boat, just as I said! I bet the boat will appear soon, and be loaded – and then chug off to the waiting ship!'

But the ship came no nearer, and no boats appeared. 'Waiting for the tide, I expect,' thought Wilfrid. 'What *will* the others say when I tell them all this! They won't believe me! And I bet they won't tell me off for going off by myself!'

He decided to go back and find the others and tell them what he had seen. He set off, trying to remember the way. Surely he must be near the place where he had left them? And then quite suddenly, someone leapt out from behind a tree and caught hold of him!

'Let me go, let me go!' shouted Wilfrid, in a panic. And then he gave a cry of relief as he suddenly saw Timmy running towards him.

'Timmy! Save me!'

But Timmy didn't coming running to save him. He stood there, looking up at him, rather puzzled, while poor Wilfrid went on struggling, really frightened!

Then Wilfrid heard a giggle. A GIGGLE? Who on earth could be giggling just then? He forced himself to look round – and saw Dick and Anne, doing their best not to laugh, and George holding her sides. His captor let go of him and began to laugh too. It was Julian!

'That's mean! You gave me a horrible fright,' said Wilfrid. 'I've already been captured once this afternoon. What do you think you're doing?'

'Where have you been, Wilfrid?' said Julian, rather sternly. 'I told you not to go for a walk –

and you went.'

'I know. I went off by myself – and a man caught me and scared me. Then I ran away and lost myself. I couldn't find any of you,' said poor Wilfrid. 'But I saw something very very interesting on that walk of mine!'

'What?' asked Julian, at once.

'Let's sit down, and I'll tell you,' said Wilfrid. 'I feel quite shaky. You really were mean to jump on me like that.'

'Never mind, Wilfrid,' said Anne, feeling sorry for the boy, who really did look rather shaken. 'Now go on, tell us everything that happened.'

Wilfrid sat down. He was still trembling a little. Everything seemed to have happened at once. He began to tell the others about the Wailing Cliffs, and all he had seen.

They all listened with intense interest.

'So *that's* the other way to the underground treasure chamber – through a passage in the cliffs!' said Julian. 'I never thought of that! That's something to know! I vote we go and explore the cliffs ourselves, when there's nobody about.'

'Well, it had better be in the evening,' said Wilfrid. 'Just in case we were spotted climbing down the cliffs to find the passage – if there is one, and I think there must be! Those men might be on the watch, now they know there's someone on the island. I bet they guess I'm not the only one – even though I told them I came alone.'

'I vote we have something to eat,' said George. 'We can talk over everything then. It's ages since we had a meal. Let's go and open some more tins, and plan what we're going to do tonight. This is getting too exciting for words. Isn't it, Timmy?'

'Woof,' agreed Timmy. *Too* exciting, he thought. Yes – and dangerous, too. He'd keep close to George that evening, as close as he could! If she went into danger, Timmy would be close by her side!

15 Julian has an exciting plan

The five children talked and talked, as they opened more tins and had a very strange meal of ham spread with fruit salad and beans. They finished up with another barley sugar each. George gave hers to Timmy who disposed of it with a crick-crack, swallow!

'Have we all got torches?' asked Julian. 'I know it'll be bright moonlight tonight, but as we'll probably be going down – or up – dark caves, we'll want torches.'

Yes – they each had a torch. Wilfrid, for some reason, had two, rather small but quite efficient.

'What's the plan going to be, Ju?' asked George, and Timmy gave a little whine, as if to say 'Yes, tell us.' He sat by George, listening earnestly, with Wilfrid on the other side of him. At times he sniffed at the baby hedgehog still in the boy's pocket, and apparently quite happy there. Wilfrid had been busy catching insects for it, much to Timmy's interest.

'I propose that we go to the cliffs – the Wailing Cliffs – as soon as it's twilight, and make our way down,' said Julian. 'There's probably some kind of pathway down, I should think – even if only a rabbit path. I'll lead the way down, of course. Anne and Wilfrid are to come between me and Dick, with George and Timmy behind.'

'Right!' said everyone.

'We are, of course, to make as little noise as possible,' said Julian. 'And please try not to send stones hurtling down the path or cliff, just in *case* anyone's about! When we get down to the rocks, we'll let Wilfrid go ahead, because he saw where the men went in and out earlier on.'

Wilfrid felt suddenly important – it was like planning an exploration! He suddenly remembered something – the wailing noise.

'I hope you won't be scared when you hear the awful wailing noise,' he said. 'It's only the wind screaming in and out of the holes and corners of the great cliffs.'

George made a scornful noise. 'Who's scared of the wind!' she said.

'Timmy might be,' said Julian, smiling. 'We

know what makes the wailing. He doesn't! You may have to hold him when it begins, George. He'll be a bit uneasy.'

'He won't!' said George. 'Timmy's not afraid of anything in the world!'

'Oh yes, he is,' said Dick, at once. 'I know something that scares him badly – makes him put his tail down and flop his ears.'

'You do not!' said George, angrily.

'Well, haven't you seen him when you speak sharply to him?' said Dick, with a chuckle. 'He goes all shaky in the legs!'

Everyone laughed except George.

'He does not,' she said. 'Nothing scares Timmy, not even me. So shut up, Dick.'

'It may be that it'll be best for only one or two of us to go right into the depths of the caves,' went on Julian. 'If so, the rest must wait in hiding. Just keep on the lookout for any signal from me. I don't expect we'll see a soul down there tonight, but you never know. If there's a way through the cliffs to that underground chamber where we saw the golden statues, we'll be in real luck. We'll then be absolutely certain how things can be taken in and out.'

'Taken *in*? But I thought they'd been there for ages,' said Dick, 'and were probably only taken out to sell. *Smuggled* out.'

'Well, I think it may be more than that,' said Julian. 'It might even be a central clearing-ground for a great gang of high-class thieves, who would hide valuable stolen goods there till it was safe to sell them. However, that's just a guess!'

'*I* think somebody's discovered the underground chamber, full of that rich old man's treasures, and is taking them out bit by bit,' said Dick. 'Anyway, whatever it is, it's very exciting. To think we know so much!'

'All because we went down the well to get some water!' said Anne.

'Put on your jumpers,' said Julian. 'It may be freezing cold in the wind that rages round those cliffs!'

'I'm longing to start!' said George. 'It's an adventure, this – do you hear that, Timmy? An adventure!'

'Anything more, Julian?' asked Anne. Julian always sounded so very grown-up when he gave them a plan of campaign. She felt very proud of him.

'That's the lot,' said Julian, 'except that we'll have some sort of a meal before we go this evening. Wilfrid will have to lead the way for us, as he's the only one who knows it – but when we come to the cliff, *I'll* lead you down. Can't have anyone missing a footstep and rolling headlong, frightening any robber or smuggler!'

'Do you hear that, Timmy?' said George, and Timmy whined, and put a paw on George's knee as if to say: 'It's a pity you haven't sure feet like mine, with rubber pads beneath, so that *your* footing is always sure!'

George patted his paw. 'Yes – you've got good sure feet, Tim. I wish I could buy some like them!'

The time seemed to go very, very slowly after that. Everyone was eager to start, and kept looking at their watches! The sun left a bright glow in the sky, so they would probably start more or less in daylight, which would, however, soon fade into twilight.

They had another meal, but strangely enough, nobody felt very hungry!

'We're too excited!' said Julian, giving Timmy a biscuit.

Timmy was the only one who didn't seem at all

excited. As for George, she fidgeted and fidgeted until everyone was quite tired of her!

At last they started off. Wilfrid led them at first, as he knew the way. Actually he found that he didn't really know it – it was the loud wind that guided him, just as it had done before.

'Very like far-off voices shouting to one another,' he said, and everyone at once agreed.

When they came near to the cliff, the sound gradually changed into the mournful wailing noise that gave the cliffs their name. 'EEE-ee-OOOOO-oo-EEEEEEEEAH-OOO!'

'Not very nice,' said Anne, shivering a little. 'It sounds as if someone is crying and sobbing and howling!'

'Good name for this place – Wailing Cliffs,' said Dick. 'Wow – what a wind up here! I'm glad my hair's my own! It'd certainly be blown off if it weren't! Hang on to Timmy, George – he's more blowable than we are – not so heavy!'

George put her hand on Timmy's collar at once. How DREADFUL if Timmy were to be blown over the cliff! He gave a grateful lick. He didn't like the wind here very much – it had a truly miserable voice!

They came to the edge of the cliff and looked down cautiously, in case anyone should be on the rocks below. But, except for some big gulls preening their feathers there, there was no sign of life.

'No boats about – no ship – nothing,' said Dick. 'All clear, Julian!'

Julian had been looking for a good path down the cliff. There didn't seem to be a continuous one. 'We'll have to go so far – then climb down a bit – then walk along that ledgy bit, see – then climb down that slanting rock – the great big one – and get down on to the more level rocks. OK everyone?'

'I'll let Timmy go first,' said George. 'He's so sure-footed and will know the best way. Go on, Timmy – lead us down!'

Timmy understood at once and went in front of Julian. He took the first little path down the cliff, slid down the next bit, walked along the ledge that Julian had pointed out, and then stood and waited for everyone. He gave a little bark as if to say 'Come on. It's easy! Follow me!'

They all followed, some more carefully than others. George and Wilfrid were least careful, and poor Wilfrid lost his footing and slid quite a long way on his bottom. He didn't like it at all, and looked quite scared!

'Watch your feet, now, Wilfrid,' said Julian. 'It's getting a bit dark, so don't try any funny tricks. You tried to *jump* over that big stone instead of stepping over carefully. I really don't want to send Timmy down to the bottom of the cliff to pick up your pieces!'

At last they were all down the cliff and on the rocks below. The tide was out, so that waves did not splash up and soak them. Anne suddenly slipped into a pool and made her shoes wet, but that didn't matter. They were only plastic ones.

'Now – exactly where did you see those men, Wilfrid?' asked Julian, stopping on a big flat rock.

Wilfrid jumped beside him, and pointed.

'See the cliff over there? See that funny rock shaped a bit like a bear? Well, that's where I saw the men. They went by that rock, and disappeared.'

'Right,' said Julian. 'Now, no more talking please – although this wailing sound would drown almost anything. Follow me!'

He went over the rocks towards the big bear-like one that Wilfrid had pointed to. The others followed, a little tide of excitement welling up inside them. Anne caught hold of Wilfrid's hand, and squeezed it.

'Exciting, isn't it?' she said, and Wilfrid nodded eagerly. He knew he would have been scared stiff by himself – but with the others it was an adventure – a really exciting adventure!

They came to the bear-like rock. Near it was a dark place in the cliff – a way in?

'That's where the men came out, Julian,' said Wilfrid, keeping his voice low. 'Do we go in there?'

'We do,' said Julian. 'I'm going in first and I'm going to stand very still and listen, as soon as I get the sound of the wind and sea out of my ears. If I hear nothing I'll whistle, OK? Then you can all come in too.'

'Right!' said everyone, thrilled.

They watched as Julian went to the dark slit-like opening. He paused and looked inside. It was so dark that he knew they would all need their torches! He switched on his powerful one and shone it into the passage. He saw a channel that ran slanting upwards for some way, and on either side a rocky ledge, not too rough. Water ran down the rocky channel and bubbled out beside him, to join the sea over the rocks.

'I'm just going into the cliff tunnel a little way, to see if I can hear anything or anyone,' he said. 'Wait here.' He disappeared inside the dark opening and everyone waited in impatient excitement.

A gull suddenly swooped down close to their heads. 'Ee-ooo, ee-ooo, EEE-OOO!' it screeched, and made them all jump violently. Wilfrid almost fell off his rock, and clutched at George. Timmy growled, and looked up angrily at the seagull. Silly bird, frightening everyone like that!

There came a low whistle, and Julian appeared again, his torch switched on.

'All clear,' he said. 'I can't hear a sound inside the opening, and I've been some way along. It's not hard going. There's a funny little stream flowing down, and a ledge either side we can walk on. Very convenient! Now, no talking please – and be careful even of your whispers – every sound seems to be magnified in here. Keep hold of Timmy, George, in the steepest places.'

Timmy gave a little whine of surprise when George took him inside the cliff. At once his whine was magnified all round them, and everyone jumped. Timmy didn't like it at all.

George took firm hold of Timmy's collar. 'You're to keep close by me,' she whispered, 'and you're not to make a sound. This is an adventure, Timmy – a big adventure – and you're in it as much as any of us. Come along!'

And there they go, all of them, climbing up the dark passage into the cliff! What will they find – what will they see? No wonder their hearts beat fast and loudly, no wonder Timmy keeps close to George. An adventure? He must be on guard then – *anything* might happen in an adventure!

16 A journey underground

It was very dark inside the cliff. The children's torches made bright streaks everywhere, and were very useful for seeing the safest places to tread. As Julian had told the others, there was a strange little stream flowing down the middle of the steep passage, with uneven ledges on each side of it. It had worn this little channel for itself during the many, many years it had flowed down inside the cliff.

'It's probably water draining from the surface of the cliffs,' said Julian in a low voice, picking his way carefully. 'Be careful here – the ledges are *very* slippery!'

'Oooh!' said Wilfrid, treading on a slippery bit, and finding one of his feet in ice-cold water.

The echo took up the noise at once, 'OOOOH-OOOOOOH-OOOOOH!' Poor Wilfrid's little 'Oooh' echoed up and down and all round them! It was very weird indeed and nobody liked it. Anne pressed close to Julian, and he squeezed her arm comfortingly.

'Sorry about my "Oooh",' said Wilfrid, in a low voice. 'My oooh, oooh, oooh!' said the echo at once, and George simply couldn't *help* giving a giggle, which at once repeated itself twenty times!

'You really will have to be quiet now,' came Julian's voice, almost in a whisper. 'I have a feeling we're coming to some big opening. There's suddenly a great draught blowing down this steep passage – I can feel it round my head.'

The others felt it too, as they climbed higher up the steep passage, trying to avoid the tiny stream that splashed down its worn channel. It made a nice little noise – very cheerful, Anne thought – and gleamed brightly in the light of their torches.

Julian wondered how on earth anyone could take crates or boxes down such a steep dark passage! 'It's *wide* enough, I suppose,' he thought. 'But only just – and the bends in it must be very awkward for boxes to get round! I hope we don't meet anyone round a bend, carrying a crate or two! Wow, the draught is quite a wind now! There *must* be an opening somewhere.'

'Ju – we've not only gone upwards, we've gone a good way forward too,' whispered Anne. 'Wasn't the old castle somewhere in this direction?'

'Yes – I suppose it would be,' answered Julian, stopping to think. 'I wonder if this passage comes up in one of its cellars! An old castle like that would have huge cellars – and probably a dungeon or two for prisoners! Let me think – we must have left the cliff behind now – and yes – I think we *may* be heading for the castle. Why didn't I think of that before?'

'Well, then – the well wall must run down beside the castle foundations!' said Dick, in much too loud a voice.

The echo made everyone jump violently, and Julian stopped climbing and hissed at Dick. 'Whisper, can't you, idiot! You nearly made me jump out of my skin!'

'Skin, skin, skin!' said the echo, in a strange whisper that made George want to laugh.

'Sorry!' whispered back Dick.

'I think you may be right about the well wall running down beside the foundations of the castle,' Julian said, whispering again. 'I never thought of that. The castle wasn't very far from the well. It'd probably have enormous cellars spreading underground.'

'The wall in the well, that the funny little door was in, was really thick,' said Dick. 'I bet I was looking into one of the castle cellars, when I peeped through it!'

This was all very interesting. Julian thought about it as they went on and on through the endless passage. It ran more or less level now, and was easy to walk through, for it was much wider.

'I think this part of the passage was man-made,' said Julian, stopping and facing the others, his face bright in the light of their torches. He went on in a loud whisper, 'Up through the cliff the passage was a natural one, very difficult to climb – but here it's quite different – look at these old bricks here – probably put there to strengthen the tunnel.'

'Yes – a secret way from the castle to the sea!' said Dick, almost forgetting to keep his voice down, in his excitement. 'Isn't it thrilling!'

Everyone began to feel even more excited – all except Timmy, who didn't much like dark, secret passages, and couldn't imagine why Julian was taking them for such a gloomy and strange walk. He had splashed solemnly through the stream the whole time, finding the stone ledges much too slippery for his paws.

The draught grew stronger and was very cold indeed.

'We're coming near to the opening where the draught comes from,' whispered Julian. 'All quiet, now, please!'

They were as quiet as possible, and Anne began to feel almost sick with excitement. Where were they coming to? Then suddenly Julian gave a low exclamation.

'Here we are! An iron gate!'

They all tried to crowd round Julian to see. The gate was a big strong one, with criss-cross bars of iron. They could easily see between the bars, and they shivered in the draught that swept through the great gate.

Dick shone his torch through the bars, his hand shaking in excitement. The bright ray of light ran all round what looked like a stone room – quite small – with a stout, nail-studded door at the far end. This door was wide open, and it was through this that the steady draught blew.

'This is a cellar – or a dungeon, more likely!' said Julian. 'I wonder if the gate is locked.'

He shook it – and it swung open quite easily, as if it had been well-oiled! Julian stepped into the dungeon, flashing his torch all round the dark and dismal little place.

He shivered. 'It's cold as ice, even on this warm day!' he said. 'I wonder how many poor, miserable prisoners have been kept down here in the cold!'

'Look – here's a staple in the wall,' said Dick, standing beside him, examining the half-hoop of iron deeply embedded in the stone wall. 'I suppose the unhappy prisoner was tied up to this, to make his punishment even worse.'

Anne shivered. 'How could people be so cruel?' she said, her vivid imagination seeing wretched men here, with perhaps only crusts of bread to eat, water to drink, no warmth, no bed, only the stone floor!

'Perhaps some of them escaped out of the gate and went down the cliff passage,' she said, hopefully.

'No – it's much more likely that the passage was used to get *rid* of the prisoners,' said Dick. 'They could be dragged down to the sea and drowned – and nobody would ever know.'

'Don't tell me things like that,' said Anne. 'It makes me think I'll hear groans and cries. I don't like this place. Let's go.'

'I hate it too,' said George. 'And Timmy's tail is right down. I feel as if this horrible dungeon is full of miserable memories. Julian, *do* let's go.'

Julian walked over to the nail-studded door and went through the doorway. He looked out on to a stone-paved passage, with stone walls and ceiling. He could see other doors, iron-barred, along a dismal stone passage. He came back to the others.

'Yes – these *are* the castle dungeons,' he said. 'I expect the castle cellars are somewhere near too – where they stored wine and food and other things. Come on – let's explore. I can't hear a sound. I think this place is absolutely empty.'

They all followed Julian down the stone passage, looking in at each miserable dungeon as they passed. Horrible! Dirty, damp, cold, bare – poor, poor prisoners of long ago!

At the end of the passage was another iron-barred door, but that too was wide open. They went through it and came out into an enormous cellar. Old boxes were there, old worm-eaten chests, broken chairs, loose papers that rustled as their feet touched them – the kind of junk that can be found in a thousand cellars! It all smelt rather musty – although, as Julian said, the draught that blew everywhere took away some of the smell.

They came to some stone steps and went up them. At the top was another great door, with an enormous bolt on it.

'Fortunately the bolt is *our* side,' said Julian, and slid it out of its socket. He was surprised that it went so smoothly – he had expected it to be rusted and stiff. 'It's been oiled recently,' he said, shining his torch on it. 'Well, well – other people have been here not long ago, and used this door. We'd better go quietly in case they're *still* here!'

Anne's heart began to beat loudly again. She hoped there was no one waiting round a corner to jump out at them!

'Be careful, Julian,' she said. 'Somebody may have heard us! They may be waiting to ambush us. They . . .'

'All right, Anne – don't worry!' said Julian. 'Timmy would give us a warning growl if he heard a single footstep!'

And at that VERY moment Timmy *did* give a growl – an angry, startled growl that made everyone jump, and then stand still, holding their breath.

Dick looked round at Timmy, who was growling again. His head was down and he was looking at something on the floor. What was it? Dick swung down his torch to see. Then he gave a small laugh. 'It's all right. We don't need to be scared yet. Look what Timmy's growling at!'

They all looked down – and saw a great fat toad, its brilliant eyes staring steadily up at them. As they exclaimed at it, it turned aside, and crawled slowly and clumsily to a little damp spot in the corner of the wall.

'I've never seen such a big toad in my life!' said Anne. 'It must be a hundred years old! Oh, Timmy, you made me jump when you suddenly growled like that!'

The toad squatted down in its corner, facing them. It seemed to glare at poor Timmy.

'Come away, Tim,' said Dick. 'Toads can ooze out some very nasty-smelling, nasty-tasting stuff. Never bite a toad!'

Julian had now gone through the door at the top of the steps. He gave a loud exclamation – so loud that the others rushed to him in alarm, wondering what was exciting him.

'Look!' said Julian, shining his torch into the dark space beyond. 'See where we've come to! Did you ever see such a storehouse of wonders!'

17 *In the treasure chamber*

Julian's torch shone steadily into the vast room, which seemed to have no end! The others shone their torches too, and Timmy pressed between their legs to see what the excitement was.

What a sight! They were actually in the enormous chamber that they had seen through the opening in the well wall! What a place it was – absolutely *vast*, thought Anne, awed at the size, the height and the great silence.

'There are the golden statues!' said Dick, going over to a group of them. 'Wonderful! Strange faces they have, though – not like ours. And look how their slanting eyes gleam when we shine our torches on them. Makes them look as if they're almost alive, and looking at us.'

Anne suddenly gave a cry and rushed over to something.

'The golden bed!' she said. 'I *wished* I could lie on one – and now I will!' And with that she climbed on to a vast four-poster bed with a great canopy, now rotting to pieces.

The bed gave a mournful creak, and the part that Anne was lying on suddenly subsided. The canopy collapsed and Anne disappeared in a cloud of dust. The bed had, quite literally, fallen to pieces! Poor Anne.

The others helped her up and Timmy looked at the clouds of dust in surprise. What was Anne doing, making such a dust? He sneezed loudly, and then sneezed again. Anne sneezed too. She scrambled quickly out of the collapsed bed and dusted herself down.

'It has a carved gold headpiece, and gold legs and end-piece,' said Dick, shining his torch on it. 'What a monster of a bed, though – I should think *six* people could sleep in it at once! What a pity it's been lost here so long – all the hangings fell to pieces as soon as Anne climbed on the bed part! *What* a dust!'

There was no doubt about it, there were priceless treasures in this vast underground cellar. The children could not find the sword with the jewelled handle, nor the necklace of rubies, which Julian thought were probably locked away in one of the chests. But they found many other wonderful things.

'Look in this chest – this beautiful carved chest!' called Anne. 'Gold cups and plates and dishes. Still bright and clean!'

'And look what's in here!' shouted George. 'Wrapped up in stuff that falls to pieces when I touch it!'

They crowded round a great enamelled box. In it was a set of animals carved out of some lovely green stone. They were absolutely perfect, and, when Anne tried to stand them up, each of them stood as proudly as once they did many years ago when little princes and princesses played with them.

'They're made of green jade,' said Julian. 'Beautiful! Goodness knows how much they're worth! They should be in some museum, not mouldering away in this cellar.'

'Why didn't those collectors take these – and the golden statues – and all the other things?' wondered Anne.

'Well, that's obvious,' said Julian. 'For one thing this is a secret cellar, I should think, and nobody would be able to get into it unless they knew the secret way to it. There's probably a sliding panel or hidden door that leads to it, somewhere in the castle above. It's very cold, and ruined in many parts – and some of the walls have fallen in – so I suppose it was pretty impossible to get to the cellars even if the secret way was known!'

'Yes – but what about the way we came up,' said Dick. 'From the sea – up the cliff passage!'

'Well – I don't know exactly why that hasn't been used before,' said Julian, 'although I can guess! Did you notice that great heap of fallen rocks near the entrance to the cliff passage? I should think that that part of the cliff fell at one time, and hid the passage completely – blocked it up. Then maybe a storm came, and the sea shifted some of the rocks – and lo and behold, there was the secret passage – open again!'

'And somebody found it – somebody, perhaps, who'd heard the old legends about the castle of Whispering Island!' said Anne.

'A collector of old things, do you think?' asked George. 'What about those two men on the island – the ones we saw in the courtyard – do you think *they* know about this entrance?'

'Yes, probably,' said Julian. 'And it's likely they were put on guard in case anyone else found it and came to rob the secret chamber. The things here are priceless! Those men aren't there to guard the animals on the island, as they were in the old couple's day. They had *genuine* keepers, like that nice man Lucas who told us about this island this morning.'

'You think these men are in somebody's pay then – somebody who knows about this great chamber under the castle, and wants to get the centuries-old treasures?' said Dick.

'Yes,' said Julian. 'And what's more I don't believe that the real owner of the island – the great-nephew of the old couple who owned it – even *knows* they're here, or that anyone is taking things from the island. For all we know he may live in America or Australia, and not care about his island!'

'How strange!' said Anne. 'If *I* owned an island like this, I'd live here and never leave it. And all the animals and birds would be protected as they once were, and . . .'

'Dear Anne – what a pity it *isn't* yours!' said Julian, ruffling her hair. 'But now, the thing is –

what are we going to do about this? We'll talk about it when we're back at the cottage. Hey, it's getting late! It'll be pitch-dark outside, unless the moon is up and the sky is clear of clouds!'

'Well, come on then, let's go,' said Dick, making for the great nail-studded door.

Then, as Timmy suddenly gave a blood-curdling growl, he stopped in fright. They had *shut* the door – but now it was opening. Somebody was coming into the great underground chamber! Who *could* it be?

'Quick – hide!' said Julian, and he pushed the two girls behind a great chest.

The others were near the golden bed and they crouched behind it at once, Dick's hand on Timmy's collar. He had managed to stop the dog from growling, but was afraid that Timmy would begin again at any moment!

A man came into the room – one of the two big men that the children had seen in the courtyard. He didn't seem to have heard Timmy growling, for he sauntered in, whistling lightly. He shone his torch all round, and then called loudly.

'Emilio! Emilio!'

There was no answer at all. The man yelled

again, and then an answer came from beyond the door, and hurrying footsteps could be heard. Then in came the other big rough man, and looked round, shining his torch. He lighted an oil-lamp on a box, and switched off his torch.

'You're always sleeping, Emilio!' growled the first man. 'You're always late! You know the boat comes tonight to take the next batch of goods – have you got the list? We must wrap them up quickly and take them to the shore. That little statue has to go, I know!'

He went over to the statue of a boy whose eyes gleamed with emeralds.

'Well, boy,' said the man, 'you're going out into the world! How'll you like that after being in the dark so long? Don't glare at me like that, or I'll box your ears!'

Apparently the golden boy went on glaring, for the man gave his head a sharp smack. The other man came over and shifted a long, deep box over from the wall to the little golden statue. Then he began to wrap it up carefully, rolling material round and round it from head to foot while the golden boy stood patiently.

'What time is Lanyon coming for it?' asked

Emilio. 'Have I time to wrap another?'

'Yes – that one over there,' said the first man, pointing. Emilio went whistling over to it, passing the chest behind which the girls were hiding. They crouched right to the floor, afraid of being seen. But Emilio was sharp-eyed, and thought he saw something move as he passed by the chest. He stopped. What was that poking out by the side of the chest – a foot! A FOOT!

Emilio rushed round the chest, his torch switched on again. He gave a loud shout. 'Carlo! There's someone here! Come quickly!'

Carlo, the second man, dropped what he was holding and raced round to Emilio, who had now pulled the girls roughly to their feet.

'What are you doing here? How did you get in?' shouted Emilio.

Julian shot out from his hiding place at once, followed by Dick and Wilfrid. George was doing all she could to hold back Timmy, who was now deafening everyone with his angry barks. He did his best to get away from George, but she was afraid he might fly at Emilio's throat. The two men were full of amazement to see the five children and Timmy!

'Keep that dog back or I'll shoot him,' said Carlo, producing a gun. 'Who are you? What do you mean by coming into this place?'

'We came by boat – but the boat got washed out to sea,' said Julian. 'We've been camping on the island. We just – er – wandered into this place by mistake.'

'By mistake! Well, I can tell you that you've certainly made the biggest mistake of your life!' said Carlo. 'You'll have to stay here for quite a long time – till our job's done, at any rate!'

'What's your job?' asked Julian, bluntly.

'Wouldn't you like to know!' said Carlo. 'Well – one part of it is to guard the island, and keep off strangers! Now, we've jobs to do tonight and tomorrow, and I'm afraid you're going to have a miserable time! You'll stay down here in this old cellar till we come back again – and what'll happen to you after that, I don't know, because I'll have to tell my employer you've been spying down here. I wouldn't be surprised if he doesn't hand you over to the police – or lock you up down here for a month, on bread and water!'

Timmy growled very fiercely indeed, and tugged hard to get away from George and fly at this horrible man. She hung on to him for all she was worth, although how she longed to let him leap at the man and get him on the ground!

'Better go, Carlo, or we'll miss that boat out there,' said Emilio, grumpily. 'We'll deal with these kids when we get back!' He shouldered the box into which he had put the wrapped statue, and started for the door. Carlo followed him, backing all the time to make sure that George did not set Timmy on to him. He shut the great door with a loud bang, and shot the bolt.

'Don't say anything for a minute in case they're listening outside the door,' said Julian.

So they all stood in silence, Anne's knees trembling a little. Oh dear – how unlucky to be caught like this!

'Relax!' said Julian at last. 'You all look so stiff and tense!'

'Well, I should *think* so!' said Dick. 'I don't particularly want to stay shut up here till those men deign to come back and do a bit more stealing. What if they *never* come back! We'd be here for keeps!'

'No, Dick!' said Anne, and to everyone's surprise, she began to laugh. 'We can *easily* escape!'

'What – through that locked and bolted door?' said Dick. 'No chance!'

'But we *can* easily escape!' said Anne, and George suddenly brightened up and nodded her head, smiling. 'Oh yes – of course! Don't look so solemn, Dick! Look up there!'

Dick looked up to where Anne was pointing. 'What am I supposed to look at?' he said. 'The old stone wall?'

'No – just there – over the top of that tall chest,' said Anne.

Dick looked – and then a large smile came over his face. 'WHAT an idiot I am! That's the old iron door in the side of the old well wall, isn't it – the opening I looked through! It looks just like an ordinary ventilation hole from down here – and I don't think anyone would ever notice it except us, who know what it is. I see what you're getting at, Anne!'

'Good old Anne!' said George, realising what Anne had in mind. 'Of course – we've only got to climb up to that hole in the wall, open the door there, and then go up the well – and we're safe!'

'Yes. But it's easier said than done,' said Julian, soberly. 'We've got to get hold of the rope, and climb right up it to the top – *not* very easy!'

'What if the rope's at the top, with the bucket hanging on the hook?' said Anne. 'We'd never reach it then!'

'We'll think of something!' said Julian. 'Anyway, it's our only hope of escape. Now – we'll push that huge, high chest or wardrobe or whatever it is, right over against the wall, under that opening into the well – there's a sturdy little one over there. Come on! We'll be through that opening in no time, and up the well. What a shock for dear Emilio and Carlo, when they come back and find that the birds have flown!'

18 A very exciting time!

It was quite a job pushing the heavy chest over towards the stone wall of the castle. It took all of them shoving with all their might, to do it.

'We seem to be making an awful noise with the chest scraping over the floor,' panted Dick. 'I hope we're not heard!'

Timmy wished he could help. He kept jumping up and pressing his paws on the side of the chest, but Dick stopped him.

'You're getting in the way,' he said. 'You go and sit near the door and warn us if you hear those men coming.'

So Timmy ran to the door and sat there, his head cocked to one side listening, while the others went on shoving the heavy chest along. At last it was in position. Then came the job of hoisting a stout little wooden table on top. Julian climbed up to the top of the chest to take the table from Dick, but just couldn't manage it, it was so heavy and solid. So George climbed up beside him, and between the two of them they pulled up the little oblong table, and set it firmly on top of the chest. Julian stood on it – and found he could easily reach the little iron door that led into the old well.

'Good,' he said, and he gave the door a hard shove.

It shook a little but didn't budge. He gave it another hard push.

'What's up?' said Dick, climbing up beside Julian. 'It *must* open – the bolt's not there any more – it fell off into the well. I expect it's rusted a little again. We'll both shove it together.'

The others watched the boys anxiously, dreading every moment to hear the two men returning. Together the boys pushed at the iron door – and it groaned and then gave way, swinging open inside the well wall! To the boys' delight, there was the rope, hanging near them!

'We've done it!' Dick called down softly to the others. 'We'll come down and help you up to the table here – then we'll try our luck up the well.'

The others were soon on the chest top. There wasn't room for everyone on the table, and Dick and Julian were debating what to do next.

'*You* go up the rope, Julian,' said Dick. 'You can climb up to the top and get out and look around and make sure there's no one about. Then Wilfrid can climb up – do you think you can, Wilfrid?'

'Of course,' said the boy. 'Then I can help Julian to wind up the rest of you.'

'Right!' said Dick. 'I'll stay here with the girls, and help each of them on to the rope, first Anne – and you two can wind the rope up, with her on it. Then George can go – and I'll follow last of all and shut the well door.'

'And when the men come they won't know how on earth we got out of the treasure chamber!' said Anne, grinning. 'What a shock for them!'

'When you've all gone up safely, I'll climb in myself and shut the door,' said Dick. 'Ready, Ju? I'll shine my torch for you!'

Julian nodded. He squeezed through the old iron door, reached out for the rope, and swung on it for a moment. Then up he went, hand-over-hand, till he reached the top, a little out of breath, but delighted to be out in the open air and the bright moonlight. It seemed almost as light as day!

He called down the well. 'I'm at the top, Dick, and all's well. Moon's out, and all's quiet.'

'You next, Wilfrid,' said Dick. 'Can you get hold of the rope all right, do you think? For *pity's* sake don't fall into the water. My torch'll give you plenty of light.'

'Don't worry about *me*! It's just like being on the ropes in gym at school,' said Wilfrid, scornfully.

He swung his legs into the opening, leapt at the rope, hung on, and began to climb up just like a monkey.

Julian's voice came down the well again, echoing hollowly, sounding rather odd. 'Wilfrid's safely up. Now send Anne – we'll wind up the rope for her so that she doesn't need to climb, only to hang on.'

Through the opening went Anne, and sat on its ledge.

'Can you swing the rope a bit, Julian?' she called. 'It's a bit far for me to jump.'

'Watch out! For goodness' sake be careful!' called Julian, in alarm. 'Tell Dick to help you.'

But the well wall opening was so small that Dick couldn't even look through it while Anne was sitting there. 'Don't jump till you've got firm hold of the rope, Anne,' he told his sister, anxiously. 'Is Ju swinging it to and fro? Can you see it clearly? It's so dark in the well, and my torch isn't too good now!'

'Yes. I can see it,' said Anne. 'It bumped against my legs then, and I just missed getting it. Here it comes again – I've got it! I'm going to hold on to it tightly and drop off the ledge. Here I go!'

She sounded very much braver than she felt. She let herself drop off the ledge, and there she swung on the thick rope, with the black water far below!

'Wind me up, Ju!' she called, and held on as the two boys at the top exerted all their strength. Dick saw her disappear up the well, and heaved a sigh of relief. Now for George.

He climbed down from the table and chest and looked for George and Timmy, shining his torch everywhere. To his utmost surprise he couldn't see them! He called softly, 'Timmy!'

A small stifled whine came from somewhere. Dick frowned. 'George – where are you? For goodness' sake hurry up and come out from where you're hiding. Those men might come back at any time! Don't play the fool.'

A dark curly head poked out from behind a large box near the door, and George spoke in a very fierce voice. 'You *know* Timmy can't hang on to a rope! He'd fall and be drowned. I think you're all horrible to forget that he can't climb. I'm staying here with him. You go on up the well.'

'Certainly *not*!' said Dick at once. 'I'll stay here with you. I suppose it's no use asking you to let *me* stay with Tim, while you climb up?'

'Not the slightest use. He's *my* dog, and I'm sticking by him,' said George. 'He'd never desert *me*, I'm sure of that.'

Dick knew George only too well when she was in one of her determined moods. Nothing, absolutely nothing, would make her change her mind!

'All right, George – I expect I'd feel the same if Timmy was mine,' said Dick. 'I'm staying here with you, though!'

'No,' said George. 'We'll be all right, Tim and I.'

Dick ran to the chest and table that he had used to get up to the opening in the well wall, and climbed quickly to the top. He swung himself through, sat on the edge of the opening and called up the well.

'Julian? Are you there? Listen – George won't leave Timmy because he can't climb up the rope. So I'm staying with her!'

No sooner had he said these words than he heard someone unlocking the door of the room they were in! Timmy growled so fiercely that Dick's heart jumped in fear. What if Tim leapt at those men – and one of them had a gun!

George heard the noise and the key turning in the door, and quick as lightning she went behind a pile of boxes with Timmy.

'Go for them, Timmy, just as soon as you can!' she said. 'Get them down before they can hurt you.'

'Woof,' said Timmy, understanding every word. He stood beside George, ears pricked up, showing his teeth in a snarl. The door opened, and a man came in, carrying a torch.

'I've brought you a light,' he began – and then Timmy leapt at him!

Crash! Down went the torch and the light went out. Down went the man too, shouting in fear as the big dog leapt on his chest, his hairy face so close that the man could feel the dog's hot breath. The man's head struck against the edge of a chest, and he was suddenly still and silent.

'Knocked out, I think!' said Dick to himself, and very cautiously shone his torch round. Yes – there was the man on the floor, eyes closed, unmoving!

George was at the open door, looking out, Timmy by her side. 'Dick! I'm taking Timmy down the secret way through the cliffs. I'll be perfectly safe with him.'

'I'll tell Julian,' said Dick. 'He's still at the top of the well, expecting you and Timmy. You go as quickly as you can – and be careful. Timmy'll look after you.'

George disappeared at top speed, her shoes making no sound. She looked anxious but not afraid.

'She's so brave!' thought Dick, for the hundredth time. 'Doesn't turn a hair! Now I'd better get back to that opening in the well, and tell Julian that George and Timmy have gone down the secret way. That man's still knocked out, thank goodness!'

He was soon on top of the chest and table, and peering through the hole. He could see the light from Julian's torch far away at the top, the light flashing on and off as if signalling. Dick called up 'Julian!'

'Oh, so you're still there,' said Julian, sounding very relieved. 'Anything happened?'

'Yes,' said Dick. 'I'll tell you in a minute. Swing the rope a bit, Ju.'

The rope swung near Dick, and he caught it, and was just about to swing himself into the well when he heard a noise. He looked back into the vast room, which was now in darkness, for he had switched off his torch.

Someone came in hurriedly. 'What's happened? Why didn't you—' Then he stopped as the light from the torch he carried picked out the figure of the man on the floor. He gave an exclamation and knelt down by him. Dick grinned to himself – what about a nice little shock for this man? He reached down to the sturdy little table, gave it a shove that sent it hurtling down to the floor, and then swung himself into the well on the rope. He

was just in time to see the table fall with a crash
by the man with the torch and to hear him shout
in fear – and then Julian and Wilfrid hauled him
up the well, still grinning to himself. 'Bit of a
shock for those men!' he thought. 'George and
Timmy disappeared – and the rest of us gone very
mysteriously! Pull, Julian, pull! I've got a great
story to tell you!'

And soon he was up on the well wall, telling
the others what had happened. They laughed in
delight.

'Good old George! Good old Timmy!'

'George knows the way down the cliff passage
all right – and if she didn't Timmy would take her
safely,' said Julian. 'We'll go down on the rocks
and meet her, I think. She should be all right
because the moon's out now, and everything's as
light as day!'

And off they all went through the wood,
laughing when they thought how puzzled and
mystified those men would be!

19 Anne is a tiger!

In the meantime, George was hurrying down the secret way through the cliffs. Timmy ran first in front and then behind, his ears pricked for any possible pursuer or danger. He could hear no one. Good! Both he and George were glad to hear the babbling of the funny little underground stream as it ran swiftly down towards the sea.

'It's a nice friendly sound, Tim,' said George. 'I like it.'

Once or twice they slipped from the wet ledges into the water, and George felt a bit afraid of falling and breaking her torch.

'It wouldn't be much fun if we had to go down this passage in the pitch-dark!' she told Timmy, and he gave a little woof of agreement.

'What's that bright light?' said George, suddenly, stopping in the passage. 'Look, Tim – *very* bright. Is it someone coming with a torch?'

Timmy gave a loud bark and rushed in front.

He knew that torch all right! It was the one that somebody sometimes hung in the sky, and that George called the moon. Didn't she know?

George soon did know, of course, and cried out in delight. 'Oh, it's the *moon*, of course, dear old moon. I'd forgotten it was a moonlit night tonight. I wonder where the others are, Timmy. You'll have to smell them out!'

Timmy already knew where they were! He had caught their scent on the wind. They weren't very far away! He barked joyously. Soon they would all be together again!

He and George came out of the tunnel in the cliff and found themselves on the rocks. The sea was splashing over them, and the waves gleamed brightly in the bright moonlight.

George saw something moving in the distance. She put her hand on Timmy's collar.

'Careful, Tim,' she said. 'Is that someone coming over there? Stay by me.'

But Timmy disobeyed for once! He leapt away and splashed through the pools, over seaweed, over slippery rocks, barking madly.

'Timmy!' called George, not recognising who was coming. 'TIMMY! COME BACK!'

And then she saw who were coming over the rocks in the bright moonlight, picking their way through the slippery seaweed. She waved and shouted joyfully.

'Here I am! I've escaped all right!'

What a joyful meeting that was! They all sat down on a convenient rock and talked nineteen to the dozen, telling each other what had happened. And then a big wave suddenly came up and splashed all over them!

'Oh no!' said Julian. 'Tide's coming in, I suppose. Come on – let's get back to Whispering Wood.'

Anne gave an enormous yawn.

'I don't know what the time is,' she said. 'And it's so bright everywhere that I'm not sure if it's day or night. All I know is that I'm suddenly really SLEEPY.'

Julian glanced at his watch. 'It's very late,' he said. 'Long past our bedtime. What shall we do – risk sleeping here on the island – or find Wilfrid's boat and row across to the mainland – and have a nice, long, peaceful snooze in that little cottage?'

'Oh, don't let's stay on the island!' said Anne.

'I'd never go to sleep! I'd be afraid those men would find us.'

'Don't be silly, Anne,' said George, trying not to yawn. 'They wouldn't have the foggiest idea where to look for us! I honestly don't fancy looking for Wilfrid's boat, rowing all the way to the mainland, and then climbing up that steep hill to the cottage!'

'Well – all right,' said Anne. 'But shouldn't somebody be on guard – shouldn't we each take a turn?'

'Why so fussy, Anne?' asked George. 'Timmy would hear anyone!'

'I suppose he would,' said Anne, giving way. 'We'll stay here then.'

They were all very tired. The boys pulled up armfuls of old dry bracken and spread it on a sheltered patch of grass, where bushes surrounded them and sheltered them from the wind. It wasn't far from the cove where Wilfrid's boat lay. They snuggled into the bracken.

'Nice and cosy!' said George, yawning. 'Ohhh! I've never felt so sleepy in my life!' And in three seconds she was sound asleep! Wilfrid dropped off at once too, and Dick and Julian were soon giving little gentle snores.

Anne was still awake. She felt nervous. 'I'd like to know if those men are safely underground,' she thought. 'I can't imagine that they're very pleased at us getting away – they'll know we'll go to the mainland as soon as we can and tell everyone what we've found! I'd have thought they'd try to stop us leaving. They must *know* we have a boat!'

She lay and worried, keeping her ears open for any strange sound. Timmy heard her tossing and turning and crept over to her very quietly, so as not to wake George. He lay down beside Anne, giving her a loving lick, as if to say 'Now, you go to sleep, and I'll keep watch!'

But still Anne didn't fall asleep. Still she kept her ears wide open for any unusual sound – and then, quite suddenly, she heard something. So did Timmy. He sat up, and gave a very small growl.

Anne strained her ears. Yes – it was certainly voices she could hear – low voices, that didn't want to be heard. It was the men coming to find Wilfrid's boat! Once they had that, the children couldn't get away from Whispering Island!

Timmy ran a little way from the bushes, and

looked round at Anne as if to say 'Coming with me?'

Anne got up quietly and went to Timmy. He ran on in front, and she followed. She really *must* see what was happening, then if it was anything important, she could run back and rouse everyone. Timmy was taking her to the cove where Wilfrid had left his boat, hauled high up on the sand for fear of big waves.

They were both as quiet as they could be. Timmy growled a little when he heard the voices again, much nearer this time.

The men had come quietly round the island in their own boat, to set Wilfrid's boat adrift. Anne saw them pushing Wilfrid's boat down the sand towards the sea. Once it was adrift, she and the others would be prisoners on the island! She yelled at the top of her voice.

'You stop that! It's OUR boat!'

And Timmy began to bark his head off, prancing round the men, and showing his big white teeth. The barking awoke all the others and they leapt up at once.

'That's Timmy!' shouted Julian. 'That's Timmy barking! Come on, quickly – but be careful!'

They ran at top speed to the cove. Timmy was still barking madly – and someone was yelling. It sounded like Anne. 'ANNE – no, no, it couldn't be quiet little *Anne*!' thought Julian.

But it was! For when the four arrived at the cove, there was Anne yelling to Timmy to bite the men, and dancing about in a rare old temper!

'How DARE you come and take our boat! I'll tell Timmy to bite you! And he will too! Get them, Tim, get them! How DARE you take our boat! *Bite* them, Timmy!'

Timmy had already bitten both the men, who were now rowing away in their own boat at top speed. Anne picked up a stone and sent it whizzing after them. It struck their boat and made them jump.

Anne jumped too when she turned and saw Julian, George, Wilfrid and Dick.

'I'm so glad you've come!' she said. 'I *think* Timmy and I have frightened them off. The crooks!'

'Frightened them off! You've scared them stiff!' said Julian, hugging his sister. 'You even scared *me*! The mouse has certainly turned into a fearsome tiger! I can almost see smoke coming out of your nostrils.'

'A tiger? Did I *really* sound like a tiger?' said Anne. 'I'm glad! I hated you all thinking I was a mouse. You'd better be careful now, I *might* turn into a tiger again!'

The men were now out of sight, and Timmy sent a volley of barks after their vanished boat. What chance had any men against a dog and a tiger? WOOF!

'Julian – why can't we row back to the mainland *now*?' demanded Anne. 'I'm so hungry and there's nothing to eat here now. And I wasn't really very comfortable in the brackeny bed. I'm longing to sleep in a *proper* bed. I've a good mind to take that boat of Wilfrid's and row myself back, if you don't want to come.'

Julian couldn't help laughing at this new fierce Anne. He put his arm round her.

'I believe it's dangerous to say no to a tiger,' he said. 'So you can have your way, Anne. *I'm* really hungry too – and I bet the others are.'

And, in five minutes' time, the six of them were out on the sea, Julian taking one oar, and Dick the other. 'Swish-swash – swish-swash' went the oars, and the boat rocked as it sped along.

'I bet if those men spot us out on the sea in a boat, going across to the mainland, they'll feel pretty worried,' said Julian. 'They'll know we'll be going to the police first thing tomorrow. This has been quite an adventure, hasn't it! I'll be glad of a little peace now!'

Well – you'll soon have it, Julian! That little cottage is waiting for you all, with its glorious view over the harbour and Whispering Island. You'll have quite a bit of excitement tomorrow, of course, when the police take you back to the island in their boat, and you show them the old well, the vast treasure chamber, the secret passage, and all the rest. You'll be there when all the men are rounded up, you'll watch them chugging off, prisoners, in the police boat, amazed that the Famous Five should have defeated them. What an adventure! And what a relief when all the excitement is over, and you lie peacefully on the hillside, with the little cottage just behind you.

'Now for a real lazy time!' said Anne, when the Five had seen the last of the police. 'Let's all go out on the hill in the sunshine, and have orangeade and biscuits and fruit salad – and Wilfrid'll play his magic pipe and bring his furred and feathered friends to see us.'

'Has he found his pipe then?' said Dick, pleased.

'Yes. He took the well bucket to get some water to drink – and the pipe was in the bottom of the bucket!' said Anne. 'He thinks it must have fallen there the last time he went to fetch water from the well – and nobody noticed it!'

'Oh *good*!' said George, thankfully. 'Wilfrid, what about playing a tune on your little pipe? I'm so glad it's found. I'd like to hear it again.'

Wilfrid was pleased. 'All right,' he said. 'I'll see if my friends here still remember me!'

He sat down on the hillside a little away from the others and began to blow down the pipe – and out came the strange little tune! At once the birds in the trees around turned their heads. In the bushes the lizards raised themselves, put their quaint heads on one side and listened. Rabbits stopped their play. The big hare bounded up the hill, its great ears taking in every note. A magpie flew down to the boy's foot and sat there.

Wilfrid didn't stir. He just went on playing as the creatures came to listen. Timmy listened too, and went to the boy, pressing against him, licking his ear. Then he went back to George.

We'll leave them all there in the sunshine, quiet and peaceful, watching the little creatures that Wilfrid can always bring around him.

Julian is lying back, looking at the April sky, glad that their adventure ended so well. Dick is looking down at Whispering Island, set in the brilliant blue harbour. Anne is half asleep – quiet little Anne who *can* turn into a tiger if she has to!

And George, of course, is close to Timmy, her arm round his neck, very happy indeed. Goodbye, Five – it *was* fun sharing in your wonderful adventure!

Special note from Enid Blyton

My readers will want to know if Whispering Island is real, set in the great blue harbour in the story – and if the little cottage on the hills is there still – and the golf course in the story – and Lucas, who tells the children about the island. Yes, the island is real, and lies in the great harbour, still full of whispering trees. The little cottage on the hills is still there, with its magnificent view and its old well – and Lucas can be found on the golf course, nut-brown and bright-eyed, telling stories of the animals and birds he loves so much. I have taken them all and put them into this book for you – as well as the friends you know so well – The Famous Five.

HAVE YOU CHECKED OUT THE FAMOUS FIVE WEBSITE?

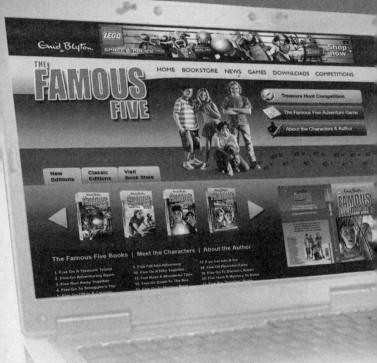

**MAKE FRIENDS WITH JULIAN,
DICK, ANNE, GEORGE AND TIMMY TOO!
ESCAPE TO A WORLD OF ADVENTURE WITH GAMES,
DOWNLOADS, ACTIVITIES AND LOTS MORE, BY VISITING**

WWW.FAMOUSFIVEBOOKS.COM

THE
FAMOUS FIVE'S
SURVIVAL GUIDE

Packed with useful information on surviving outdoors and solving mysteries, here is the one mystery that the Famous Five never managed to solve. See if you can follow the trail to discover the location of the priceless Royal Dragon of Siam.

The perfect book for all fans of mystery, adventure and the Famous Five!

ISBN 9780340970836